EM
X

"Can't we part with dignity?"

Lauren continued her desperate appeal to his reason. "Otherwise I'll be in danger of... hating you!"

"If you're prepared to hate me on such petty grounds," Dale replied, "then perhaps I should give you real cause to hate me—hmm?"

She shuddered back from him as he reached for her and took her into an iron-hard, loveless embrace. His breath was hot upon her cheek, but when he claimed her lips she knew it was only to humiliate her.

To be in his arms by force was sheer torment, a denial of the very purpose of such closeness. And yet she strained to him, clung, almost enjoyed a moment of rapture that would not last, nor be remembered except with a recoil of shame....

JANE ARBOR
is also the author of these
Harlequin Romances

Many of these titles are available at your local bookseller.

For a free catalogue listing all available Harlequin Romances
and Harlequin Presents, send your name and address to:

HARLEQUIN READER SERVICE,
M.P.O. Box 707, Niagara Falls, NY 14302
Canadian address: Stratford, Ontario N5A 6W2

One Brief Sweet Hour

by

JANE ARBOR

Harlequin Books

TORONTO • LONDON • LOS ANGELES • AMSTERDAM
SYDNEY • HAMBURG • PARIS • STOCKHOLM • ATHENS • TOKYO

Original hardcover edition published in 1980
by Mills & Boon Limited

ISBN 0-373-02419-3

Harlequin edition published August 1981

CHAPTER ONE

THE windswept mercantile dock of a South Wales harbour on a February afternoon was an unlikely setting for adventure. But Lauren had eyes only for the sleek white ship alongside, the pleasures of which she had bought at the price of discarding prudence and economy and all the other rainy day precepts she had obeyed for so long.

She would have to abide by them again, of course. There would be a coming back, but all that was for tomorrow. The name of the game immediately ahead was *luxe*.

The taxi had set down on the dock her three matching blue hide cases; a ship's porter snatched them up. At the head of the gangway Lauren was met by a white-clad steward, and she was aboard *Chaconia Lady*, one of a very few privileged passengers in a ship of the Halcyon Line of private freighters on the West Indian run—periodically east with a full cargo of tropical fruits; west from England, carrying general merchandise to the islands.

Only a fortnight earlier she had seen her dream of lap-of-luxury travel destroyed by a clerk in Halcyon's London office. He had laughed to scorn her presumption that she could hope for a passage so late. No, nothing foreseeably ahead either. Halcyon vacancies were like gold dust, didn't

Madam realise? Lauren was left with the impression she had tried to rent an apartment in the Vatican or the White House, and had not trusted at all the man's vague promise of 'Should we have a cancellation, we'll ring you.' Cancellations of anything you wanted too badly didn't happen. He wouldn't ring.

But he did. An outside cabin on the passenger deck of the *Chaconia Lady*, sailing from Barry Docks on the 19th inst., had unexpectedly become available. Madam would kindly confirm by telephone and letter that she would take it. Madam had confirmed . . .

There were flowers and fruit, courtesy of the Line, in the cabin. The furniture was upholstered in silver-grey tweed, the bed covered in blue and silver quilted silk; there were wide portholes, a generous wardrobe, a coffee table and a desk. There was a silver-grey tiled bathroom 'off'. They would sail shortly before dinner, her steward told her. Would she prefer to rest now, or be shown the other amenities laid on for the passengers' diversion on board?

Lauren elected to see them—the sundeck under a half awning, the swimming pool, the bar, the dining saloon, the lounges—the palatial hotel in miniature which she had pictured as her home for the ten days or so of the voyage. She would leave it for an equally plushy hotel on the island of St Just, for another fortnight's stay, and after that —— Well, after that she would fly home by the cheapest bargain flight which offered. In less than a month she would have spent more money than should suffice for half a year. But at this end of the enterprise she didn't care.

She had bought clothes to match the rest of her extravagance—evening things, play shorts and pants and halter-tops, a light topcoat, a walking suit, headscarves and sandals; had spent time and too much money on make-up lessons and had had her cap of blue-black hair styled and swirled about her face.

Not that much could be done for her face, she told her reflection in the mirror of her cabin dressing-shelf. More heart-shaped, it could have passed for 'piquant'. As it was, it was merely pale and slightly hollowed below the high cheekbones perhaps of some far-back Slav ancestor of whom she had no knowledge. Her nose was a little aquiline, making a clear-cut profile with her short upper lip, narrow chin and the long line of her throat. Black eyebrows tilted at each outer corner; eyes, green in a good light, were raven-black in shadow——

Dale had once teased her—'Put you in a red and orange bandanna, give you a coconut-shy to manage, and you could pass for a Romany any day.' Steven, so far as she could remember, had rarely praised or blamed her looks, even in fun——

Dale; Steven—both behind her now. Now she was Lauren Napier and alone. Doing her best with a tolerable figure and ordinary features with a gipsy cast. Neither expensive chic nor a veneer of poise could make her beautiful, but briefly she was going to savour their effect.

The afternoon had darkened. There were lights

everywhere now, on the dock, in the sheds and all about the harbour. There was a busyness on board. Several cars had arrived, unloaded their passengers and their luggage, and driven away. The full muster was to be only twelve, Lauren understood. Eleven wealthy people—they had to be wealthy to travel by the Halcyon Line!—as yet unmet, and in ten days or so's time, as good as never met, when she and they had gone their separate ways. How long would any of them remember her except as the young widow who had travelled out alone in Cabin Number Nine?

One did not dress for the first night at sea, so she chose a bolero-jacketed black suit, touched with prim white at wrists and collar. She made up with less daring than her instructor had said she could afford, but brushed her hair to the big one-sided curve the stylist had achieved for her, after scorning the demure centre parting with a light fringe which she had worn for years. The change had lent her a sophistication she had not had before.

There was a judder underfoot and the throb of the diesels changed. *Chaconia Lady* was under power as Lauren made her way to the lounge bar where she supposed people gathered before dinner. She took her dry sherry to a table and watched those who came in.

It developed into a cocktail party of seemingly kindred souls, introduced or reunited to each other by the First Officer, a bearded redhead. For at least one couple knew another. For them both the journey was a going-home to Barbados;

they had met on the eastward voyage. There was a doctor returning to St Just, two West Indian business men and a honeymoon couple bound for a tour of the Caribbean. Ten of us down, two to come, thought Lauren as she was swept into the friendly circle.

She listened, tried to memorise names, answered questions and learned facts. Doctor Gellhorn had been on a course in London and was eagerly returning to his practice and his French wife. The honeymooners were bubbling with questions about the West Indies, and the Barbados people were ready to answer them. Lauren asked some herself too; this was also her first trip out, she told them.

Once, when the talk was general, it turned on the subject of the Line. 'A remarkable improvement since the takeover,' remarked one of the West Indians.

'Yes, indeed,' said someone else. 'Let's see, when *was* that?'

'Two years, three. It was a touch of genius to buy in the Line and make a monopoly of the freightage and luxury passenger clientele at a stroke. Must have cost a few million, though.'

'Chickenfeed to them, by all accounts. Wise, to keep the name Halcyon. What better to lure the sun-starved English to the certainty of getting some?'

'And have they been lured!' put in the honeymooner. '*We* had to time our wedding to the chance of getting passages on this voyage, nine months ago.'

Someone else said, 'I hear we're to be honoured

by the Old Man himself on this trip. Or—' counting heads— 'perhaps by him *and* his careerist son, as we seem to be two under strength so far.' But dinner had been announced before either of the absentees had arrived, and when they did, one was an elderly English lady who joined Lauren and Doctor Gellhorn and one of the West Indians at their table for four, and the other was a man for whom a place had been kept at the Captain's left hand.

Mrs Scruby-Gould was particular as to the placing of her chair, and not until the dining-room steward had it just right, with the lighting on her left, did Lauren notice the man, his hand on the back of his chair, but still unseated as he looked the company over before bending to speak to the Captain and then sitting down.

Lauren had stared, her blood seeming to congeal as the cool glance had raked her, appeared to dismiss her and moved on. *Dale!* Dale Ransome— here, in an inescapable proximity she would have given worlds to be spared. (Or would she?) He was too far in her past. She had grown out and away from him, married another man, known widowhood. If only—if only!—that unknown hadn't cancelled his passage, he would have been travelling in her place, and the shock of Dale wouldn't have happened to her. And yet was she so sure that he was nothing to her now, that she really would have preferred the Captain's guest to be someone else, and Dale lost and forever in the world of her past? She did not know.

Doctor Gellhorn's voice came to her through a

drumming like the onset of a faint. 'So the grape-vine got it wrong. It's the young one, not the old one, lighting back on the trail by sea instead of by air. Usually claims he hasn't the time for deck-quoits and jogging, but I suppose the occasional finger on his pet project is necessary. Have you met Dale Ransome, Mrs Napier?'

She could have lied, but there seemed no point. 'Oddly enough, I did meet him a long time ago. I knew his family were in importing then, but I'd heard nothing since about what you were discussing before dinner. Is it true they took over the Halcyon Line at some time or other?' she asked.

'Yes, but not until a long while after they'd specialised in importing tropical fruit, grown under their own name in the islands. Then they used other firms' freighters, while Halcyon paddled back and forth as a lesser cruise-line, gradually losing its patronage to air travel. That was when Dale came up with the idea of buying in Halcyon cheap, refrigerating and dolling-up its fleet of six vessels, and making us eager customers help to pay for some of the best refrigeration in the world. Getting it going took a couple of years and Halcyon has been afloat in its present form for more than another two. And it's always been Dale's baby, as you can imagine.'

'I see. And does the firm still operate from London, or from where?'

'Oh, in London, the Headquarters. Somewhere far down in the City.' (Lauren could have told him where.)

'I booked my passage from the Halcyon office

in Pall Mall. I didn't know about the Ransome connection,' she said.

'No. Halcyon is for the paying public; Ransome mostly for the trade.' Doctor Gellhorn went on, 'Dale commutes back and forth as and when necessary, but he chooses to live on St Just, in a house not far from my own.'

'Is he—married?' The question came with difficulty.

'No, though the island ladies have him in their weather-eye. He keeps a cook and a houseman, as most of us do, and his brother Oliver lives with him.'

'Oh—yes, I remember he had a younger one, though I didn't meet him. Is he in the firm too?'

'No, he's barely eighteen and a patient of mine.' Medical etiquette stopped Doctor Gellhorn there, and he asked instead, 'How and where did you happen to meet Dale, then?'

Lauren said, 'On holiday in the south of France. It was my first time abroad and just after I'd qualified in physiotherapy. It was all of five years ago—he wouldn't be likely to remember me now.'

The doctor looked at her with professional interest. 'Physiotherapy, hm? Useful. Do you still practise?'

'Not since early in my marriage. I'm widowed now.'

'Yes, I know. We heard so on the coconut radio—Caribbean for "grapevine"; in plain English, busybody gossip,' grinned her companion. 'Meanwhile—' he threw her a look of gallant admiration—'I doubt very much that Ransome can have forgotten you. We shall see.'

He did his duty then by Mrs Scruby-Gould, while the other man claimed Lauren's interest in a potted history of the islands' changing fortunes through the centuries.

She listened, said, 'Is that so?' and 'Really?' at intervals, but her mind was not with him or his story.

The doctor was right—Dale couldn't wholly have forgotten her. They had parted in anger and bitterness and had not looked back. She had not dared to, lest she run to him, only to be torn apart again. And he could not have wanted to, for he had not come. They had not met again, but they had had their hour of wonder and discovery and delight in the desire they had sparked in each other, and at their age then—he had been twenty-five, she just twenty—such wounding as they had later done to each other must surely have left scars?

Yes, Dale could not but remember her. Just now, before he sat down, he had given no sign. But face to face with him, she was going to dread far more the dagger-thrust of his recognition, than if he had genuinely forgotten her and showed her only the cool appraisal of a stranger. It was too much to hope—wasn't it?—that, remembering her indeed, he had also forgiven her?

It was. After dinner, when a few people wrapped up for a stroll on deck, while the others, Lauren among them, repaired to the lounge, she knew he must have seen her, though he stayed at the bar, talking to the other men there. She had thought the doctor might have broken the ice for them by bringing them together, but he was not in sight, and it was not until Lauren rose, meaning to go to her cabin, that, though his back was to her, Dale seemed to sense her movement and came over to her.

'Mrs Napier?' was his sole greeting to her. So he had been primed to her change of name either by the Captain or the passenger-list. She nodded an unnecessary Yes, and he went on in a lower tone, 'We have to talk. Will you come to my cabin?'

'To your——? No, thank you. I'd—rather not,' she said.

He frowned and swirled the whisky in the glass he held. 'I'm privileged,' he said. 'I have a suite big enough and public enough to hold a party in it. But if you're afraid of assault, we can always leave the door open. Please come.'

It was typical of the masterly assurance she had admired in him that he should assume she remembered him enough to be persuaded to obey him without question; she guessed he knew he did not need to taunt her into compliance, that though his order sounded like a polite invitation, it was an order all the same. And always in the old days, he had only to say 'Come', and, eager and willing to make his will hers, she would follow. He hadn't the right to expect it of her now, but she went with him all the same.

He had not changed. Before they had actually met at play on the St Raphael shore, she had dubbed him in her mind as 'the brown man'. And he was that still; brown-haired, copper-tanned, long limbs moving with athletic ease from the hip, the torso now hidden by his shirt, a golden glow of smooth flesh and rippling muscle, she knew. His eyes were blue and deep-set. At moments of dry amusement or raillery, an eyebrow had a trick of lifting at the same time as a corner of his mouth. But the trick was not in evidence now. When they reached his suite, the look he turned upon her was one of clinical appraisal, no more.

She took the chair he offered her, shook her head at the gesture he made towards a drinks tray. He remained on his feet, one leg bent backward at the knee to support him against a mahogany fitment for drinks and books. He said, less as an opinion than as a fact, 'You've changed.'

Lauren supposed she could have replied with an arch, 'Do you think so?' but knowing the trouble and expense of her new image must show to anyone who had known the old Lauren Kenyon, she agreed simply, 'Yes.'

He studied her face, the draped line of her hair. 'As effective as you could have wanted and the beauty boffins could make you,' he commented. 'How long since?' And then, before she could answer, he nodded towards her wedding ring. 'How long since that, anyway?'

'Something over two years ago.'

'Who was he?'

'His name was Steven. He died last July.'

Dale said, 'I'll do the conventional thing if it helps, and say I'm sorry. But do I take it he fostered the change during his reign, and was able to buy it all handsomely for you?'

Lauren thought quickly. Suddenly ashamed of her peacock escapade, she could not bear to confess it to his relentless grilling; pride forbade her to admit to the reckless one-off operation which had left her bank balance barely in credit. Let him conclude that her grooming and the clothes he would see her wearing on this fabulously expensive trip were part of her everyday way of life. She said quietly, 'I'm afraid Steven was often too ill to notice what I bought or wore.'

'Too *ill*?'

'He died of the leukaemia he'd contracted four or five years before. We met when he was a patient in the hospital where I was working.'

Dale frowned as he worked it out. 'Then you married him, knowing he suffered from it?'

'Yes.'

'Why?'

'Considering all things, have you the right to ask?' she countered with sudden spirit. 'I had my own reasons, and one of them was pity for him.'

'*Pity?*' Dale's echo was an explosion. 'You had the consummate nerve to *marry* the fellow for pity? He had the right to it from just anyone, or he could buy it from a nurse, couldn't he? Or he could have had it from you by the basinful as a friend. But to humiliate any man by marrying him for pity alone——!'

'You don't know that I didn't love him as well,' Lauren defended.

Dale shook his head. 'No. If you had, you wouldn't have missed the chance to throw it in my face.'

'You think that after all this time I would bother?'

'To get back at me? Certainly, even after all this time. Being a woman, you couldn't resist it,' he said with conviction. 'However, how come you were working when you met your man? Don't tell me milady stepmama had so far loosened her grip on your misguided loyalties as to allow you to take a job away from home?'

Lauren scorned, 'You don't gain anything by petty sarcasm. No, I was able to work at the local hospital from home. But at last she'd agreed to go to her sister-in-law in Canada on a visit, and when I wrote to her about Steven she was terribly hurt, she said, and that if I were thinking of marrying him, she doubted if she could bear to come back.'

'But you begged her to—naturally?'

'Of course. After all, when Father died, he had made her my charge. She'd never been strong, and she depended on me, and I was letting her down——'

'Uh-huh, Lucille Kenyon, frail as a gathered daisy when she wasn't getting her own way,' Dale commented. 'She'd always known how to twist the screw on your devotion to her, hadn't she?'

'I suppose she was rather—demanding,' Lauren allowed.

'Demanding! She battened on you. I'm surprised you had the spirit to tell her to do as she pleased about coming back.'

'I—I didn't. I told her that if she really wanted to come back, I would break with Steven. But then she said she would stay where she was for a while, as Vancouver suited her very well, and her sister-in-law had more time than I'd chosen to give her.'

'A new victim and a pleasant climate. Also a chance to tell everyone that her stepdaughter didn't want her. And so you went ahead and married Steven Napier?'

'Not at once. Some time later.'

'Hoping she'd change her mind and come back?'

'No, but——' Lauren broke off, reluctant to confide to him how forlorn and useless she had felt, bereft of her charge of the self-centred, tyrannical Lucille, and how, gradually, Steven had appeared as a responsibility she must take on in its place. By marrying him without loving him, she might have wronged him, as Dale had said. But then Steven had given little sign of loving her either. He had only wanted a resident nurse ...

Dale was looking at her with something near pity. 'My God, you're a glutton for punishment, aren't you? Rid of a vampire, you take on a mill-stone. What runs in your veins, woman—a solution of duty with a mixture of martyrdom? What happened to the girl I fell in love with, and who said she loved me? Or am I wrong, and she didn't exist even then? Could she only "love", or imagine she knew what it was about, as long as she was out from under stepmama's shadow? Back under it, and the man in her life could go hang. As I went hang, when I'd have done anything for you, taken you anywhere—for love! But no, when I wouldn't share you, that was it. We were finished. Finished, that is, if *you'd* ever even begun!'

The pity she thought she had read in his eyes

could only have been mock. The mounting bitterness of his tone showed that, and she shrank physically from him when he levered himself from the fitment and came over to look at her more closely as he went on, 'And so, what now for you? If you don't find another lame duck to cherish, are you going to settle for a mere hair shirt?'

She said shakily, 'I did what I thought was right—both times, when I let you go, and when I married Steven for the pity that you choose to scorn. And—and you have no right to berate me just because coincidence has thrown us together. I didn't know anything about your connection with the Line, and if I'd chosen another cruise we might never have met again.'

Dale's eyes narrowed shrewdly upon her. 'Warning me not to suspect you of following me up for auld lang syne? Well, I don't. I doubt if you've enough human sentiment to hanker for the might-have-beens of an old affair. But a coincidence that you are here and I am—no. I'm travelling by way of my job; *you* are my captive audience for the trip because I arranged it that way.'

Lauren stared at him. '*You* arranged it? How?'

'You didn't see me, but I happened to be in our West End office when you were refused a booking. Lady, name of Napier, expecting Halcyon passages to fall like heaven-sent manna, the clerk told me when I'd watched you go. So—Napier, not Kenyon, and a haute-couture chic? I ordered that you get your booking. It was as simple as that. Ransome's own the Line.'

'They—they told me it was through a cancellation. But why?'

He shrugged. 'Curiosity. You could say I do have enough human interest to want to know what happens next in a story, even when it doesn't concern me any more.'

'You didn't want to see me, but just to know what had happened to me since——?'

'Since, besotted fool that I was, you were my sun-up and my sun-down and all my day in between? Yes, I questioned—Why Napier? Whence the rather obvious wealth? And what next in view? More Lady Bountiful stuff, as I've said, or the Merry Widow kicking up her heels in escape from bondage? You're not working now, I take it?'

'Not at the moment.'

'And you're booked to St Just? Where are you staying?'

'At Le Marechal, for a fortnight.'

'H'm—five-star rating. It figures. What made you choose St Just?'

'I'd heard it was the most picturesque of the chain.'

'You must allow me to give you some introductions.'

'Thank you,' she said, 'but Doctor Gellhorn has promised me some, and I shan't have so very much time.'

'And when you go back, what will it be—bridge parties in the stockbroker belt, or a bijou apartment near Harrods'?'

'I don't play bridge, and I shouldn't want to live right in Town.' This catechism Lauren found as pointless as it was impertinent, guessing he would only snub her if she attempted one of her own, questioning him on his personal affairs. She went on, 'I suppose you wouldn't credit that I might go back to work?'

'In what you trained for—physiotherapy? I should doubt it; you've probably enjoyed the fleshpots for too long,' he said, watching her as she stood, expecting him to step back to give her room.

But he did not move, even at her, 'Please——?' Very close to her, he studied her intently. 'Unless,' he ground out, his voice very deep, 'the ministering angel bit is still your favourite image of yourself—more important than anything a man could give you or you could give a man. Prink to the last eyebrow-hair and dress to the latest whatever, and I think I'd still back you to put do-goodery before anything else——'

'If you've *quite* finished summing me up in a series of well thought out clichés——' Lauren cut in on his pause. But he cut in on hers with,

'No, I haven't finished yet,' and pinioned her with a grip on either upper arm. 'I've still this to say—God help you, if you ever do meet a man who can teach you what it is to have fire springing in your blood instead of cold gruel, and having taught you, couldn't care less what you do with the experience. For that's what you deserve, Lauren—*Kenyon*—to *want* and be denied. But will you ever, I wonder? Want *this* . . . and this . . . and this——?'

As he spoke his arms went round her and he punctuated each emphatic word with a long pulsating kiss on lips and throat and eyes, while he crushed her to his body, making her gasp for breath.

The years rolled back for her. Dale used to kiss her so—and more so—and she had answered him as she could. But this was only a questioning of which he had already decided the answer; a blaming, a taunting, and, sick with shame and anger, she struggled free.

He did not try to keep her. 'That was despicable!' she panted.

'Yes,' he agreed. 'But it proved a point, didn't it?'

She scorned to reply and turned away. 'I've rumpled your hair-do,' he said, and as he saw her out. 'Perhaps I should have left the door open after all.'

CHAPTER TWO

DURING the sleepless hours of that night Lauren questioned over and over what about their encounter had enraged Dale most. Angered him to the point where, having promised her they could as well have talked in public, in the end he had not been able to keep his contemptuous hands off her.

Was it the mere fact of her marriage? Or her motive for it, which he claimed could only have diminished Steven as a man? Or his relived anger over her refusal to desert her stepmother? Or his resentment of a show of wealth which he judged she could only have inherited from Steven?

In turn her tortured thoughts answered each question.

She and he had parted long since. So hadn't she the right to marry someone else? And couldn't he appreciate the compassion, if not love, for which she had married a man with probably only a limited time to live? And hadn't she as much cause for bitterness over their parting as he had? He had forced her to choose between Lucille and himself; if he had loved her enough to fight for her, there must have been *some* way in which they could have reached a compromise. But compromise hadn't been good enough for his male pride to accept. His ultimatum had been marriage or nothing. And Lauren's care for Lucille and Lucille's

23

self-interest had seen to it that there had been nothing.

It had been her own fault, of course, that she had let him see her as a spendthrift of money she could only have got from Steven. But that had been her own pride momentarily standing up for itself. It showed she had achieved something which had forced his notice, and in the three weeks or so ahead—even if they had to meet on St Just, which they might not—she reckoned she could put up a front which would continue to deceive him. There was no reason at all why he should ever know that her bid for luxury had been a gesture of revolt against all the drab years of life with Lucille and Steven, and had been made possible by cash from a single life policy she had not known Steven possessed. He had been that kind of a husband—secretive and withdrawn. They had lived on a small private income he had, and there had been virtually nothing to come to her but the unexpected windfall which she had already spent or budgeted for in her present defiant fling in the face of her future.

All the crowding questions answered—but still no nearer to understanding Dale than before their meeting . . . understanding least of all his impulse to those punishing, mocking kisses. He could have been moved to shake her or to slap her face if physical violence had been a need his anger couldn't resist. How had he known that to kiss her in *that* way, without feeling, was the ultimate revenge he could inflict?

For, persuade herself otherwise as she might, his

touch and his nearness could still thrill her, rousing sleeping passions to new hunger for him. Put him behind her? Her first shocked sight of him had told her she never had, and she had longed for the remembered ecstasy of moving into his eager arms, impatient to wrap her about. It wouldn't happen, of course. At any time since they had parted he could have found her again if he had wanted to. But he had only contrived to see her again when he had been able to make her his captive audience to his contempt of her. Ten days of enforced proximity to him! And to think that she could have chosen any other cruise from any other agent, instead of to the exotic West Indies and to the particular island he had chosen for his home!

Chaconia Lady was a long way down Channel when Lauren went to breakfast in the dining-saloon. The weather was still grey and most people seemed to have chosen to breakfast in their cabins, as only Mr Cave and Mr Willis, the two West Indians, were there with her. Afterwards she wrapped up and went for a walk round the main deck, took a book from the library, looked at the as yet unfilled swimming-pool, and went to the lounge to read.

Every time one of its doors opened or people passed by its windows, she looked up nervously. Any one of them might be Dale, who for form's sake would have to greet her as if nothing untoward had happened between them last night. And it was going to be like that for the rest of the voyage—a frigid politeness between them. Would people notice the necessary arm's length distance at which they kept each other? she wondered.

Dale did not appear, but later in the morning she was joined by Mrs Fremayne, one of the ladies returning to Barbados. Indicating the dank mist which hung almost to sea level, she promised Lauren, 'It won't be long like this,' and settled down to her petit-point tapestry and to talk.

'All the men in the bar were intrigued when Dale Ransome carried you off last night and you didn't come back,' she announced. 'Mr Cave, who does business with Ransome's and knows Dale well, said he could always be trusted to make a direct line for the smartest and prettiest woman on board—which undoubtedly you are, my dear, this trip. But when he—Cave, I mean—went on to say, not very nicely, that Dale was safe in knowing that a ten-days' romance with a passenger committed him to nothing, Doctor Gellhorn floored him by saying he knew you and Dale were old friends; that you'd told him so at dinner.'

'Not close friends now,' Lauren corrected quietly. 'We hadn't met for years, and for instance, I didn't know he would be travelling on this voyage out.'

'No, I gather even the Captain doesn't always know when he or the Old Man—that's his father—may suddenly decide to go one way or the other by sea instead of by air. But isn't that nice for you, dear, that you and Dale can keep each other company as the only really young people, except for our honeymooners, on this trip?' Mrs Fremayne beamed.

Lauren murmured, 'Though I daresay it has to

be a business trip for him, and that he won't have much spare time for mixing with us, will he?'

'Oh, he'll make time—if he wants to. What man can't?' Mrs Fremayne claimed airily. 'And there are always evenings and cabin parties, you'll see.'

The sociable custom on board was that the passengers should 'circulate' between tables for meals, so that for lunch Lauren found herself sitting with Mr Cave and the honeymoon couple, whose contribution to any general conversation was practically nil. Mr Cave, however, made up for them with almost continual chat to Lauren, and he had none of Doctor Gellhorn's inhibitions on gossip, for he related to her details about Dale's private life at which the doctor had stopped short, and of which she had heard nothing at all from Dale himself.

'Lovely place Ransome has there on Mont Michel,' chattered Mr Cave. 'Overlooking the harbour, with a bathing creek of its own, grounds like a park. Manages to keep his gardeners too. The house—*so* long—' Mr Cave extended expressive arms—'one-storied, of course, as houses have to be for our hurricanes—and then an attached cottage at one end of it, for his brother. You've met his brother too, Mrs Napier?'

'No, I haven't, though I knew he had one.'

'Ah. Well.' Mr Cave seemed to debate with himself what he should say next. It emerged as, 'A bad business, that. Boy came out to stay with his brother for a holiday, six months or so back, at the time of our rains. Hired himself a racing car; burned up the island roads in it; risked his own neck every day, and then had his spine or some-thing shattered when brother Dale was driving and the car overturned.'

Lauren drew a long breath. 'And——?' she questioned.

'Ransome wasn't hurt himself. The boy was taken to Barbados for surgery and was mended after a fashion, but was left with one of his legs minus feeling, owing, they say, to a vital nerve having been cut in the course of his various opera-tions. So back he goes to Mont Michel, Dale's place, and there he is still, with no sign of his being anywhere else, as far as one knows.'

'But shouldn't he have gone back to England, perhaps for further surgery to cure the paralysis of the leg?' Lauren queried.

'Should have done, no doubt. But apparently he refuses to budge; won't co-operate with Gellhorn for any treatment of the leg, and seems prepared to live on Dale in the cottage annexe to the house which Dale has turned over to him.'

'With a nurse to look after him?'

'No. They tried that, but the girl didn't last a week. So Dale's woman cooks for him and Dale's houseman serves him, and he—well, I suppose he just sits.'

'And so it's a kind of deadlock while the boy refuses treatment or to leave St Just?'

'Deadlock is right,' her companion agreed. 'You'd think his father or Dale could deport him back to England, but he's of age, and it could be that Dale has a conscience about him.'

'A—conscience?'

'Well, he was driving the car, wasn't he?' argued Mr Cave. Judging Dale for an accident he might not have been able to avoid, thought Lauren in a surge of sympathy for a burden of guilt she couldn't wish for anyone, least of all for Dale who had her heart.

She took afternoon tea with the other ladies and afterwards was on her way to her cabin when she met Dale face to face. She was prepared just to speak and to pass him, but he did not stand aside for her in the narrow corridor.

'I was hoping to see you,' he said. 'Will you dine with the Captain in his suite tomorrow night?'

'With him in his suite? Why me?' she asked in surprise.

'Just a custom of the trip. He reckons to dine all his passengers privately during the voyage. He ropes them in, two by two, like the animals in the Ark, and makes a foursome with Bill Stellhouse, his Number One on this run. Will you come?'

'Shouldn't I wait for him to invite me himself?'

'He won't. He's invited me, and I'm asking you as my guest.'

Lauren looked away. 'After last night, when you left me in little doubt of your opinion of me, that surprises me considerably,' she said.

'Why should it?' Dale retorted coolly. 'I'm entitled to what I think of the person you've become——'

'*And* to express it quite as crudely as you did?'

He shrugged. 'Once expressed, it can soon be forgotten. "Water off a duck's back"—and all that. You're headed the way you mean to go, and in a very few days of the new worlds you're setting out to conquer, you'll have difficulty in quoting what I said or did last evening to make you so uptight today.'

'I doubt it. You were deliberately offensive. But what do you mean—about new worlds I want to conquer?'

'Well, don't you?' he parried. He paused to look her over, his appraising eyes travelling from her Yves St Laurent headscarf to her sailor blouse over tapering slacks and the Gucci handbag slung over her arm. He gestured, 'All this—your London clothes, the studied chic—don't tell me it isn't directed at something or someone that's been out of your reach so far?'

She managed a laugh. 'And how wrong can you get? And if you're going by my clothes—of which you've seen very few—I suppose it doesn't occur to you that a woman with money enough to spend on them dresses to please herself?'

He shook his head. 'It isn't only your clothes. It's your air.'

'My *air*? Of what?'

'Difficult to define. But I think—of a predator long cheated of its prey, and now at last primed and ready for the kill.'

Lauren withdrew her questioning eyes from his. How far from—and yet how near—he was to the truth! How far, that she had designs on nothing nor no one tangible; how near, that she had bought with her windfall such spoils and privilege as she had never thought to own, and never would again, once the money was spent. She said tautly,

'You're still being offensive, and so no, I think I won't accept the Captain's invitation to dine with him in his suite.'

'You won't? That makes a difficulty for me.'

'Why? You can invite someone else.'

'Suppose you quote six from those available? Don't you realise you and I are the only two genuinely unattached passengers on board? All the others either have their life partners along, or are tied by a kind of umbilical cord to those they've left behind them, or are returning to. Doctor Gellhorn, Cave, Willis—and do you think I should be condemned to Mrs Scruby-Gould as my guest instead of you?'

His light, rueful tone of appeal encouraged Lauren to laugh for the first time, genuinely, in his company. She said, 'If she's to have her turn with the Captain, *someone* will have to invite her.'

'Someone, some time. But not this. Captain K. is expecting you as my guest.'

'How could he, before you'd asked me?'

'He suggested himself that, of the sample on offer, you must be my obvious choice. So that if you refuse to come, I lose face.'

'Which would never do for a *Ransome*, would it?' she taunted him, not sure now whether they were fencing with the foils on or off.

Dale gave no sign of having heard her. 'Or I carry you along by force, in which case *you* lose face,' he said. 'You will come?'

While she was dressing for the evening Lauren had told herself that while she had courted danger in letting him persuade her, there must be safety in the company of Captain Kitchin and his second-in-command. Dale could hardly snipe at her in front of them, and though his 'obvious choice' wasn't flattered to be chosen from so short and unpromising a list, she thought she could rely on his urbanity to cover up his true opinion of the woman he had decided she had become.

Guessing that dinner with the Captain in his suite was probably a social highlight of the voyage, she had chosen the most striking of her evening outfits, a long-sleeved dinner gown in white crêpe with silver embroidery at its waist and mandarin collar, and had been rewarded by the momentary, if reluctant, look of admiration on Dale's face when he called for her at her cabin. Captain Kitchin's welcome had put her at once at ease, and with his First Officer making an attentive fourth, the party had quickly got under way to connoisseur-selected wines, excellent food, unobtrusive service, amusing talk and a headily flattering regard for Lauren as the only woman among three men. She found herself enjoying it, responding to it, and not even the knowledge that Dale's contribution to it was bogus had been able to spoil her evening's success.

At the end of it she wondered if the Captain—like Royalty!—would withdraw first. But Bill Stellhouse solved that one by excusing himself for duty at the same moment as Dale's raised eyebrows had signalled that they should leave too. She had murmured her thanks, Dale had added his on behalf of them both, and now they were on their way back to her cabin to which, still conscious of a sparkle and vivacity in her mood that oughtn't to be wasted, she didn't want to go; didn't want to be alone.

The weather was gradually improving. There had been glimpses of sun that day, and on this, their third night out, there was a dead calm and the sky had cleared to a moonless dark, pricked through with stars.

Dale took his guiding hand from beneath her elbow in order to point to them. 'Care to finish off the evening in the traditional way, with a stroll on deck?' he suggested.

She hesitated and played for time. 'It could be cold,' she said.

'You could fetch a wrap.'

She hesitated again—this time not long enough for her caution to prevail. 'Very well, I'll get one,' she said.

'I'll come with you.'

He stood at the door of her cabin while she slid the partitions of her wardrobe, but he came inside to help her into the light mohair cloak she chose. The big shawl collar could double as a hood, and as Dale lifted it forward for her from behind, she was acutely aware of his nearness. If she dared to risk rejection or a repetition of that first night's humiliation, she had only to turn about to find herself breast-high to his heart ... She thanked him, shrugged cosily into the wrap and did not turn.

On deck they walked a little, then leaned, elbow to elbow, at the rail on the leeside. Presently Dale said, 'Your sophistication must be used to it by now, but you were a distinct success tonight.'

'Was I?'

'You know it. You had Kitchin and Stellhouse eating out of your hand. And that without fluttering your eyelashes at them or using any of the little-girl tricks. They genuinely liked you.'

'Thank you kindly. I'm glad I—pleased.'

He ignored the irony she intended. He went on, 'Seems that the good Steven, for all his handicaps, was good for your morale. When we parted you were a mess of jumbled emotions that made you your own worst enemy. You were as stubborn as a mule and as immature as a half-opened bud. When I tried to talk some reason into you, you might never have heard of it. But evidently Steven Napier had the edge on me. He taught you to grow up.'

And so he did, if to grow up was to expect little and to get less from the man she had married—whether it was money or companionship or love—thought Lauren. Aloud she said, 'I'm five years older now, that's all.'

'And wiser. And harder. The emergent swan, in looks and poise and an all-things-to-all-men manner—the lot.' Dale turned to set his back to the rail, so that he was facing her. She muffled her face deep in the softness of the wool and stared down into the water, letting him talk.

He said ponderingly, 'You know, I wonder you didn't choose a wider canvas for your art than a freighter on a ten-day voyage to one of the smaller of the Windwards. For instance, only eleven other passengers to bedazzle, and a smattering of crew. I'd have thought a world tour would have given you more scope, if your object were another marriage to some man you could mother.'

'Had I to have an "object", just because I chose a holiday which sounded attractive in midwinter?' she parried.

'No, but as I've told you, I think you had one.'

Perhaps because that was truer than he knew, she resented it.

'Assuming, on three days' meeting, that you know a great deal about me, and having not a qualm about catechising me on the rest? Suppose we shift the interest to you for a while instead?' she challenged. 'For instance, I know nothing about you that I haven't heard from other people on board.'

'Most of it tuppence-coloured?'

'How can I tell, when you've told me nothing yourself? Doctor Gellhorn told me you have a house on St Just where your brother Oliver is with you, and one of the West Indians, Mr Cave, told me something about the trouble that's kept him there.'

'So that, as I'm sure you can get someone else to give you a rundown on my work and my recreations—including my amours—what else do you need to know?'

Lauren recoiled at the overt snub. 'Nothing at all that you don't want to tell me,' she said.

'Well, how much of it concerns you, after all?'

'None of it,' she agreed, but feeling he needed paying out for the brusquerie of that snub, she added, 'But I forgot—I did hear too that you conduct your amours with admirable discretion, keeping them brief and without any strings.'

If she expected to offend him she was disappointed. He laughed and affected eager interest. 'Really? And if that's so, aren't I to be congratulated? For wouldn't you agree that the sign of the successful philanderer is his skill with the "goodbye-honey-so-nice-to-have-known-you" kiss?' he urged.

'And that's how you see yourself—as a philanderer?'

'It's evidently how your informants see me, though I would quarrel with them over "amours" in the plural. For I assure you, hand on heart, I've only ever conducted one at a time!'

Lauren despaired. She had asked him about himself in all sincerity, and this facetious raillery hurt like an insult. Feeling she had had enough, she straightened from the rail and drew the wrap more closely about her. 'Shall we go back?' she asked.

At the door of her cabin she said, 'Thank you for the evening,' and offered him her hand. With a totally unexpected old-world gesture of lifting it to his lips, he met her eyes provocatively.

'Keeping you up to date, currently I'm not conducting even one affair of the heart, and Nature is supposed to abhor a vacuum,' he said.

Lauren jerked her hand free and tried irony again. 'What a pity for you! Has your technique slipped, or what?' she insinuated.

'I hope not. I try to keep it primed. No, I was

only giving you fair warning.'

'Warning? Of what?'

'To the effect that if we continue to flock together, Nature, in the shape of our fellow passengers, will begin enjoyably to link our names. You can't think how they'll love to debate whether or not you have designs on me, or whether your virtue is safe from me.'

She hated the cynicism of that; it was part of the stranger Dale had become. She said, 'I don't believe you. I find people a good deal kinder than that, and mostly they only gossip out of an interest to which they have a right. But there's no problem really, is there, so long as we avoid each other's company? No one is going to have to fear for my reputation at your hands if we're seen together as little as possible. Or not at all—by choice.'

'And you think that's possible within these confines?'

'It needn't be *im*possible, given the will,' she maintained.

'With all eyes agog for a shipboard romance—admittedly with no future to it—but just a pleasant dalliance to watch to pass the time? You wouldn't cheat our friends of speculating on that by keeping markedly out of my way?'

She glowered at him. 'If I thought anyone was hatching the idea of a romance between you and me, I'd make a point of always cutting you dead on sight,' she declared fiercely.

'Even though that might be taken as a sign that we'd had a steamy lovers' quarrel——?'

But at that Lauren's patience gave out. He was

baiting her for the mere sake of it. 'So what are you trying to prove?' she flung at him. 'Do you *want* to embarrass me with people, lest they should be talking about me? Or do you want to be thought so irresistible that you can have a shipboard affair with any woman you choose—even me?'

Dale sighed elaborately. 'All this because I thought you should know that, placed as we all are, and you undeniably the most striking figure aboard, it's inevitable that people will talk!'

'It's *not* inevitable,' she denied. 'By keeping clear of you for the rest of the voyage, I can make it impossible!'

He stood aside, leaving her free to go into the cabin. 'You're welcome to try. But I'm afraid you'll have them all backing their own guess as to which of us slapped the other's face, and why,' he said.

And of course it wasn't possible to avoid him. They met in the table-changing routine of meals; they were roped into card games in the evenings, invited to cabin parties, and the poolside was a rendezvous on which most people converged for drinks and talk during the mornings, and where absences were sure to evoke comment. Whenever any pairing had to be done, their names would be suggested in almost the same breath, and in agreeing to partner Dale with as much grace as she could, Lauren was only too aware of his unspoken comment of 'What did I tell you?'

Meanwhile she was counting the days to the end of the voyage, her head calculating how long she had to wear the false front of wealth and world-liness which Dale had forced on her, and her heart betraying her by dreading the coming time when she would not see him daily walking towards her, causing her breath to catch with a desire which had nothing to do with her reason's need to forget him.

Her years with the self-centred Lucille and the unresponsive Steven had made her something of a loner, reluctant to make a confidant, but needing one now, she found she could talk more willingly to Doctor Gellhorn than to anyone.

Indirectly they were of the same profession, and he showed such real interest in her future plans that she found herself confiding to him more than anyone else knew of her.

He had said of her marriage and the wealth he supposed Steven had bequeathed her, 'It's always such a pity when medicine in any form loses people like you. *We* could diagnose till we're out of breath, but where would we be without practising nurses and therapists of all kinds to make the diagnoses work and prove us right?'

Lauren agreed, 'Yes, I was sorry to give up work. But my husband was a full-time job while he lived.'

The doctor said, 'Of course, that's understood. And now there's no need for you to practise again?'

'Not——' She had been about to lie 'Not really', but stopped, causing him to question her pause. 'Well—that is——' She hesitated again. 'The fact is, I must.'

'Must?'

'Yes.' She fought the indiscretion of telling the truth to anyone who knew Dale well, but the indiscretion won. 'You see, my husband had very little to leave me in his will—just the proceeds of one life policy, and I spent that, or shall have done, on this trip—clothes for it and so on—and on my holiday at Le Marechal on St Just. So that when I go back to England, and I shan't be going by Halcyon, I shall have to start again at square one——' She broke off with a diffident laugh. 'You must think me a reckless fool—or worse.'

'No,' her companion said gently. 'Only very human, and very feminine, and very brave. You wouldn't believe how many people would do the same, if they had the courage to face the consequences. Thank you for telling me. We've all been supposing you to be Mrs Midas or Mrs Croesus or the widow of some modern tycoon——'

'And please,' she cut in quickly, 'let them—the others—go on believing it, will you? I must have been mad to try it and to think I could carry it off indefinitely. But as far as they're concerned, it will only be for the next few days. I shan't have to meet any of them again. So please, for my silly sick pride's sake, need you tell them?'

'I certainly needn't. But you'll probably meet some of them after the end of the voyage—Dale Ransome, for one.'

'I don't have to!'

'I've told you, he's a neighbour of ours, and his brother is my patient. Do I take it that you've kept your forgivable little secret from him too?' At her nod of assent, 'You have? Then it looks as if you'll have to keep it for the length of your stay, doesn't it?'

'If I have to meet him at your house or anywhere, you will help me?' she pleaded.

'Of course. Though you know, after we'd learned you two had met before, we all had you lined up for a budding romance. You paired off so nicely—right age group, right background, both as handsome as they come—that I've even had to promise to keep the others posted as to the happy outcome if it happened before you left St Just. But I suppose that's a pipe-dream? You wouldn't have kept up the fiction with Dale if there were anything serious between you?'

Lauren said quickly, 'There's never been any question of that. We paired off, as you call it, usually because it's worked out that way—the marrieds, and the honeymooners, and you three men who know each other, and Dale Ransome and me. But it's meant nothing. We shall still part almost as strangers, and I should hate any stranger to know such an idiotic thing about me.'

'Then, as you've admitted it to me, may I argue from that that you see me as a friend?'

'Yes,' she smiled gratefully at him, 'please.'

'Good.' He looked at his watch. 'Got to keep a date with Willis in the bar.'

They had been sitting in low chairs on the sundeck, and as he stood, Doctor Gellhorn put down a hand to take hers and stooped to drop a kiss on her cheek. 'Best of luck to the "lady richly left",' he quipped kindly, and almost ran into Dale as he turned away.

They greeted each other, 'Hi!' The doctor went on, and Dale came to stand by Lauren's chair, his foot on a rung of the other.

'I'd have thought you'd know better than to play outside your league,' he commented. 'You'll probably find plenty of single ones to work on at Le Marechal, whereas Brian Gellhorn is married to a wife he adores, didn't you know?'

Lauren looked up at him, guessing he had seen and misread the trivial kiss. 'Yes, I know it,' she said. 'He sees to it that everyone does.'

'And so?'

'And so,' she said slowly and firmly, 'he's the outgoing type who kisses aunts and acquaintances and babies alike.'

'And touches, and holds hands? Has he kissed you before?'

She managed to make a yawn. 'Not that I re-member——' She stood, picked up her book and perched her cartwheel straw hat at an absurd angle on the back of her head. Bolstered by Doctor Gell-horn's promise to support her deception, she felt she could afford to flout Dale's waspish sus-picions. 'I'm going for a last swim in the pool,' she told him. 'Shall I see you there?'

'Later, perhaps. But it needn't be your last swim. We're changing course, calling at Barbados before going first to St Just. That means another night aboard.'

'Oh? Can you do that?'

'We frequently do, when our cargo demands it. We shall dock in the morning and sail again in the evening. That will give you passengers a day's sightseeing around Bridgetown.'

'But—' Lauren frowned—' my hotel on St Just—they'll be expecting me.'

'They won't. We radio when we're not docking to schedule, and all the hotels are prepared. But we can radio Le Marechal specially, if you like?' Dale offered.

'No, it doesn't matter.' She lingered for a moment, wondering whether he might suggest showing her Barbados. His absurd dog-in-the-manger warning about Doctor Gellhorn had irked her, and she would relish refusing him, even if she wasn't looking forward much to exploring a strange tropical town alone.

But with the virtual end of the voyage and half the passengers leaving the ship in Bridgetown, evidently he saw no further need to 'pair' with her merely to keep the social numbers even. Their brief masquerade as willing companions was over. He did not offer.

The next morning, as always to welcome a ship into port, there were crowds on the wharves and jetties of Bridgetown's New Harbour. On flat Barbados there was no backdrop of mountains to the shore scene, but there was overall greenery and colour everywhere. Garden colour, sky colour, white beach colour and the weathered limestone colour of the buildings. The crowds on the jetty wore colour and waved it—handkerchiefs, headscarves, even flowering branches of shrubs were pressed into the service of seeing *Chaconia Lady* in.

Of course everyone on board was also on the

rail, waving indiscriminately back. Or not entirely so. The two Barbadian resident couples had spotted their relatives and were waving to them and calling messages. And Dale, a yard or two along the rail from Lauren, had just lifted a hand in answer to a similar signal from a woman who had stepped clear of the crowd to the edge of the jetty and was looking up.

From that angle her figure was slightly foreshortened, but Lauren saw she was tall, wearing white, the perfect foil to her perfect tan. Her silver-blonde hair was drawn severely back from her face and teased into a mass of curls below the combs which held it. The effect was as of an aureole about her head. She was a beauty.

She and Dale proceeded to dumb show. She pointed to the dock buildings. He nodded and, turning, went below. Lauren's clasp upon the rail tightened, as she worked it out.

That girl had come to meet Dale. They had arranged it. But until yesterday, according to information straight from the Captain's mouth, the intention had been to dock at St Just. And so Dale, who had offered glibly to radio her hotel, had been able equally to radio Barbados and to make a date with this girl.

He had said he wasn't involved romantically with any woman. So who was she? And what were they to each other? Lauren would have given a great deal to deny that she cared to know.

CHAPTER THREE

THERE was nothing sinister or frightening about Bridgetown to a woman exploring it alone. In fact, Lauren found it engagingly English, with the added bonus of brilliant sun, and palms for dappled shade, and the lilt of West Indian voices sounding happy, even if they were not.

As always at the end of a journey, the late fellow travellers separated quickly, closely concerned with each other no more. Lauren did not see Dale or his friend in the Customs shed; Doctor Gellhorn had an appointment to keep in the town; the returning Barbadians were surrounded by a posse of relations, and Mrs Scruby-Gould was driven away in a chauffeured Rolls-Royce. Lauren strolled about the streets, watching the shoppers, marvelling at the displays of luscious fruits in the market, and shopping for a piece or two of island pottery and hand-embroidered cottons.

At noon everything quietened, the people dispersed when the shops closed and on the tree-lined square where Lauren paused, debating where she should eat, practically the only other signs of human life were the taxi-drivers drowsing at their wheels in the shade while they waited for fares. One of them, a young man with a shining chocolate face, drove over to Lauren.

'Taxi, lady? Tour of island? See sights? Hotel to eat? Beach?' His accompanying grin almost split his face.

Lauren said, 'In fact, I was wondering where to have lunch.'

'Ah—hotels Victoria, Regal, Mount Gay, Sam Lord's Castle——?' he reeled off.

She had read of historic Sam Lord, planter-turned-smuggler who had built his castle and his fortune from luring rich cargoes on to his reefs instead of their reaching safe anchorage in Bridgetown. 'Sam Lord—yes, take me there,' she said. 'Is it far?'

'Out of town. Across island, lady.' He looked as if he thought he might lose her as a fare.

'Never mind. Take me,' she said. She could afford plenty of time before *Chaconia Lady*'s deadline for sailing, and the price of just such sightseeing trips was what she had come abroad to afford. The taxi was an open four-seater and she chose to sit beside her driver, which seemed to please him. He introduced himself as Rico Morgan. 'Call me Rico.'

He spoke English well if economically, missing out any words he didn't seem to find necessary to his meaning. On the way he enlarged on the story of Sam Lord, his crimes, his wealth, his castle-turned-hotel and its ghost. Lauren found it a gracious building of high arched doorways and deep embrasured windows. In its modern sphere, to judge by the number of cars parked in its courtyard, it was evidently a popular place.

Rico drew up in the heavy shade of some trees,

and must have been puzzled when Lauren did not at once alight, though he had opened the door for her.

Head down, she made a business of fumbling for money for him in her big straw shoulder-bag. As Rico had stopped, she had seen a figure she would always recognise—Dale's. He was leaving the hotel by the main door she would have to use, and he was not alone. The stranger of the jetty was with him, an arm tucked under his. Lauren continued to fumble and to remain seated until, beneath her lashes, she saw them go to a long American car and drive away. The girl, not Dale, was at the wheel.

Rico asked mournfully, 'Finish, lady? You go back town, 'nother taxi?'

'No.' The last thing she wanted was to be the first of the passengers to get back to the ship. Particularly she would like to time her return to be just right to give the impression to Dale that she had spent an entirely enjoyable and successful day. 'Wait for me, will you?' she asked Rico. 'You could show me some of the rest of the island? I should like that.'

She gave him some money for his own lunch and from his beaming thanks and smile, she judged she had made a friend.

Her meal was leisurely and exotic. Leisurely, because, as she was to learn, almost all service in the Caribbean was done at the stroll rather than the gallop, and exotic because of the strange dishes on offer.

She chose the melon-like paw-paw as a starter,

followed by crisp bite-size flying fish, and as a main course took a concoction of chicken and saffron, with honeyed banana toasts for dessert, all new to her, as was her first taste of a genuine Caribbean rum punch.

She found Rico ready to suggest a tour—of mile upon mile of the sugar-cane of the great estates, each with its 'great house' of fine early plantation architecture; of palm-fringed beaches and modern developments such as distilleries and the airport, finishing up in Bridgetown itself, with its central savannah, a riot of floral colour, as a 'must'.

Lauren warned him of the time when, without fail, she must be back at the docks. 'Fair enough. Will be there,' he grinned.

As they drove they chatted. Rico was curious about England; she was curious about everything he could tell her or show her, and it was while they talked and compared that she felt lonely for the first time. There should have been someone to whom to recount all this—as, in the old days, she would have taken to Dale any story of a day she had spent apart from him. Now there was no one.

At one point Rico asked, 'You married lady, lady?'

'Not now,' she said, 'I'm widowed. Are you a married man?'

'No.' She had expected that—he looked so young. But then he added without embarrassment, 'I got five children and sweetheart gal.'

'Oh,' was all Lauren could find to reply, and when he went on cheerfully, 'Get married Easter, or maybe Christmas. Time enough.' She changed

the subject to ask if they were now on their way
back to the town. They had traversed so many
roads and tracks of this strange territory that she
had completely lost her bearings, but the sun was
beginning to sink, and if the tour were to last
much longer she could be in danger of missing the
deadline of eight o'clock at the docks.

When she pointed this out to Rico and showed
him her watch, he reassured her. 'Not far now.
Must see savannah and Admiral Nelson on his
monument,' he insisted, at which Lauren, envisag-
ing the park he had described, took a firm line.

'I've seen Nelson, and I'm afraid I must miss the
savannah,' she told him.

His face fell. 'Want you see my piccanins too,'
he said wistfully, and pointed ahead. 'House just
by. There? You see?'

Lauren followed the line of his finger. 'You live
out here? We're coming to your village?'

'Not village. Two/three houses, that all.' He
pulled up at one of a shanty group built of wood
and iron sheeting and roofed with a mixture of
tiles and slates, and Lauren, having bypassed a
visit to the savannah, decided she could humour
him by meeting his brood and his 'sweetheart gal'.

She smiled and got out of the car. 'Just for a few
minutes——' she began, and stopped as the door
of the first shanty creaked open and a handsome
young West Indian woman plunged out.

She ran to Rico, beating at his chest with her
fists and clamouring in a mixture of *patois* and
English. Rico held her off by her wrists and told
Lauren, 'It is our little one, our baby. Will you

come, lady?'

The open door had released four brightly pina-fored youngsters to the outside, where they stood about, eyeing Lauren in wonder until they spotted the taxi and began to climb about it. To their blasts on its raucous horn Lauren went into the house with Rico and the girl. Rico addressed her as Judy.

In a basket crib on the living-room table was a baby of a few months, Lauren judged. It was whimpering tearlessly but continually; its knees were drawn up to its stomach and its face was suf-fused. Lauren noted the knotting of muscles in arms and legs and looking at Judy for permission, took the rigid little body on to her lap on a chair which Rico cleared of a jumble of toys.

Judy managed tremulously, 'I undress her for bed, and sudden she go all—all hard, like that. You understand, lady?'

Lauren said, 'I don't know. I think so. I hope so.' She looked about her. Useless to demand a bath, h. and c., but she must have warm water deep enough to take the child to its armpits, and when she asked for it, it was provided from a caul-dron on a wood-burning stove. She supported the baby in a tin washtub, and with the towel pad she asked for, applied it, soaked again and again in cold water, as a pack to the top of the head.

Fifteen ... twenty minutes passed. On her own work in the children's wards, Lauren had seen enough cases of convulsions to be confident she was giving the right emergency treatment. But when the other children drifted in and stood about, watching her, it was unnerving to seem to fail so much trust, when the baby gave little sign of response.

At last there was some reward. The little legs relaxed and straightened and her face was a more natural colour. Lauren took her from the bath and dried her. 'It could happen again. She should see a doctor. Can you call one?' she asked Rico.

He shook his head. 'Take into hospital only. See doctor there, in town.'

'Well, take her tonight. Or no, take her in with us now.' Lauren's glance at her watch had told her that if it were true that the town was 'not far', and the detour to the hospital did not take long, she should just about make the ship's sailing time. But only just.

It was an hour and a half later, dark and nearly an hour over her deadline, when Rico pulled up on the dock.

His 'not far' had proved to be several miles; there had been a wait at the hospital, and though she could have dropped him and taken another taxi, she was late even then, and on the principle of being hanged for a sheep, she had waited with him until she was able to give her own version of the baby's spasms to the nurse and doctor who took charge of her. Perhaps, Lauren had argued to herself, the sailing time chalked on the board at the ship's rail wasn't as rigidly kept as all that, and returning passengers were accorded a little grace.

Rico, contrite and grateful, refused to be paid for the tour. Parleying with him and insisting he keep the Caribbean dollar notes she pressed upon him took some more time, and when she dashed up the gangway the warning board was still there, but so was Dale, the last person she could want to catch her in the act of what he could see as a flagrant disregard of shipboard rules.

Evidently he did, and he was not alone. As he advanced upon Lauren his day's companion moved from his side with a murmur of, 'Spare me the post-mortem, do. I'll see you in the saloon, Dale, before you do sail—O.K.?'

He nodded and let her go. To Lauren he indicated the board. 'Can't you read?' he demanded. 'Or do you simply choose to ignore a ruling it doesn't suit you to obey? Or—being really charitable—do you have a good reason for holding us up? We're not in competition for the Blue Riband, but we do have a schedule to keep, you know.'

The iciness of his sarcasm appalled her, and that girl had known he meant to berate her! And he had no right. He might be the owner of the Line, but Captain Kitchin was the ship's skipper, and it was surely his sailing schedule she had held up, not Dale's? At sight of him (just happening to be on deck or lying in wait for her?) she had had every intention of explaining and justifying herself in detail. He could not but understand about the baby—no one could, she had argued then. But now she would *not* be cowed by his pre-judgment of her without a hearing. The thought of fawning to him with an apology he shouldn't ask of her was anathema.

'As a matter of fact, I have a very good reason, I

think,' she said. That was all. But as she made to thrust past him to go below, he caught at her wrist, staying her.

He said, 'If it's as good as all that, you shouldn't mind giving it.'

'I'll give it to Captain Kitchin, not to you.'

'Then if I were you, I should wait until he asks you for it. I reported your arrival when I saw you on the dock, and to volunteer it when he's on the point of sailing wouldn't be the essence of tact.' Dale's glance raked her, making her conscious that her hair had been ravaged by the wind in the open taxi, and her nursing of the baby had left her trouser suit rumpled and none too clean. 'One could suspect you of having taken a roll in the hay, but I suppose you'd claim the benefit of that doubt. However, why go looking for the disaster of whatever befell you by taking yourself off alone?'

'There was no one else to go with.'

'I heard Willis and Cave making up a foursome with the two lovebirds. You could have kept with them. *They* arrived back on time.'

'And I didn't. Too bad!' She deplored the flippancy, but couldn't resist adding more to it. 'I'm surprised you're so bothered. I'd have thought you'd be only too thankful that in a few hours' time you'll no longer have to escort me for form's sake or to police me or even to see me again,' she said.

He shrugged and released her wrist. 'I shouldn't be too sure of that. St Just is a small island; Le Marechal is a public place where I often entertain guests, and I daresay St Just isn't far behind Barbados in offering hazards to foolhardy young women who think they know it all. Neither of them is England with street lamps and telephone booths every few hundred yards. So policing and even rescue could be necessary for loners who don't watch their step,' he warned.

Embarked on this verbal fencing, Lauren had to go on. She widened her eyes at him, evoking no softening of his granite expression. 'Don't worry,' she urged. 'I'm to have just thirteen days on St Just, and for that time, when I'm not going around with the herd, I expect I can live the life of a cloistered nun.'

'Which wasn't, one gathers, the original object of the exercise?'

Gravely, sincerely now, she said, 'No, it wasn't,' and left him before he could ask, 'Then what was?' For if he had, her defences against him would have crumbled. She would have thrown herself on the mercy of a love which he had for her no longer, admitted to his indifference that she didn't now know. Ever since that stab of loneliness she had felt that afternoon, she had wondered and would continue to wonder what happiness or reward she had hoped to gain from her mad one-off throw of extravagance of money and brief experience.

Hadn't she looked beyond the short time she would enjoy it? Hadn't she foreseen the loneliness it would mean? If Dale had asked his question with any kind of friendly interest, she would have broken down before him, told him the truth about her empty masquerade, admitted the innocent facts of the day's happenings—even have shown him that for her nothing had changed, that her body could still ache for him, her blood still fire; that she wanted him, needed him, longed for him to need her.

But this Dale Ransome was not the one she had known five years ago, one who would tease any foolishness, praise any courage—*understand*. This Dale had no pity in him, and to abandon every pride before him and be rejected was more than she could bear. The masquerade must go on. Thirteen days had never appeared so long.

The cycle of table-changing had come full circle to bring her and Doctor Gellhorn together again, and at dinner, not caring whether Dale heard it secondhand, having failed to wring it out of her, she told the doctor what had delayed her in keeping the sailing deadline.

He listened, was interested, told her she had done the right thing by the baby and made little of it as a crime. 'I've known one of the Line's skippers to hold back a sailing for a duchess who'd lost her keys and ultimately found them in her pocket. I shouldn't think Captain Kitchin will have you on the carpet for this.'

There was a festive, sentimental air to the last night on board. A good deal of champagne was drunk, and when it looked as if the party would go on for a very long time, Lauren decided to leave it while she was still sober enough not to risk oversleeping and so missing her first sight of St Just which she had been promised at dawn. She evaded various gallant offers to see her to her cabin and escaped to someone's spirited rendering of 'Will

Ye No' Come Back Again'? Her last sight of Dale was of him leaning on the bar, aloof from the small crowd surrounding her.

And yet, as she unlocked the door of her cabin, somehow he had managed to be at her heels, and when she opened the door, the doorway framed his bulk.

He had been drinking as much as anyone, and if he were drunk she feared his mood. In order to switch on the light she had had to step back into the cabin, and he followed her. 'I'm tired, and I'm going to bed. What do you want?' she asked.

'Nothing you might have been hoping for—from anyone other than me.' His voice was not slurred and his gaze at her was steady. But she distrusted his purpose in following her so furtively. After their acrimonious exchange before dinner, he had surely to be drunk to want to renew it.

She said quietly, 'That's insulting, and it doesn't tell me what you do want. So what is it?'

He answered her question with another. 'Why didn't you tell me what was your "good reason" for being late on board?'

'I suppose, because I didn't think you had the right to question me, nor to hector me when I didn't tell you,' she said.

'As much right as Brian Gellhorn, whom you did tell.'

'Only when he asked me out of interest, not as my inquisitor.'

'Your silly pride and your umbrage against me wouldn't let you tell the truth which you must know I should have had to accept?' he challenged.

She nodded. 'That's right—my pride. But as you've obviously heard it all from Doctor Gellhorn, what do you want with me now? To go on quarrelling about it, or to apologise for doubting my word?' Thinking desperately that she had to get him out of her cabin somehow, she went on in deliberate scorn of whatever drink-induced maudlin impulse had sent him, 'Because, do you know, if you've realised you behaved like a petty tyrant and want to ask my pardon, I'd appreciate it so *very* much more if you did it while you were— sober?'

At once she saw her mistake in taunting him, read it in the flash of anger which lit his eyes. He moved a step nearer to stand over her. 'Say that again and you'll be sorry,' he muttered.

Lauren stood her ground. 'Say what again? Imply that if you weren't drunk, you wouldn't be acting the boor like this, forcing your way in here, threatening me? For goodness' sake, we're within less than twelve hours of never having to meet again after we dock in the morning. For the few days I'm on St Just I shan't seek you out, and I'm sure you won't want to seek me. But at least you might let me remember that we parted with reasonable dignity, instead of my being in danger of—of hating you?'

It had been a desperate appeal to his reason, and it failed. He said, 'If you're prepared to hate me on as petty a ground that you think I've come creeping in apology, only because I'm drunk, then perhaps I should give you real cause to hate me, and to remember about me just what you please when I've done with you—hm?'

Terrified now, she shuddered back from him as he reached for her. She stifled to a gasp the cry of fear which was ready in her throat when he took her into an iron-hard grip which was no embrace but an intent to punish through pain. His compulsive mastery of her was all animal, she felt; a physical, overpowering force she could not hope to match. He had taken her into his arms, but for no purpose of love. His head was bent to hers and his breath was passionately hot upon her cheek, but when he took her lips, parting them to the false seduction of his own, she knew it was only to humiliate her and bend her to the will of his male brute strength.

When she struggled, there was a jeer in his short laugh. When she protested, 'Don't ... don't! You're hurting me!' he eased his hold, but allowed his hands to wander to her throat, her hair, her breasts, the swell of her hips imprisoned against his.

Now, as he had promised, she had reason to hate him. But now so firm was his stance, so controlled his every studied touch and movement, she knew he was not drunk, and what was more, that her body, if not her will, was melting to a ravishment which Dale meant only to be cruel.

To be for the second time and the last time in his arms by force was sheer torment, a denial of the very purpose of such closeness, a near-rape of her senses which should and did appal her. And yet she strained to him ... clung ... even almost enjoyed a moment of rapture which would not last, nor be remembered except with a recoil of shame.

When she turned her face away he brought it forward again with a hard pressure of fingers and thumb at her jaw, studied it dispassionately and chose his own time for releasing her. There was insult in his cool lack of hurry, in his pulling down of his jacket, his whole air of dusting off his hands after a job accomplished.

He said, 'Anyone who saw me follow you will be agog for results by now. What shall I tell them? That we "aren't speaking" any more? Or shall I leave it to you to prattle to Brian Gellhorn that I took advantage of you in my cups and my future name has to be mud? Meanwhile, Bon Voyage to wherever you're headed, and you're right—given the will otherwise, there's no reason why we need meet again.'

Nor did they before *Chaconia Lady* docked the next morning. After a sleepless night, Lauren was on deck when the ship stood off the harbour and the heights of the island were swathed in a dawn mist.

From the sea it was more picturesque than Barbados, more hilly, more wooded almost down to its shoreline. Above the busyness of the small port, its buildings were perched on levels along the hillsides, dotted about in the greenery as if flung there by a random hand. The shoreline was a ragged edge of bitten-in coves frilled with gently creaming foam. No desert island—its commercial front belied that—but at that hour its hinterland might have been uninhabited, for all the stir or sign of life which showed.

Other people, but not Dale, had come on deck, the homecomers like Willis and Cave and the doctor to seek and point out landmarks, the honeymoon couple and Lauren to stare in expectant excitement. At Lauren's side Doctor Gellhorn said, 'Your Arcadian landfall at last—do you think you're going to find it worthwhile?'

She knew what he meant. She turned to him with as eager a smile as she could manage. 'I hope so. From here it looks delightful—all I'd imagined. By comparison, at first sight Barbados was almost ordinary.'

He leaned on the rail. 'Yes, so we Justinians, by adoption as well as by blood, like to think. We live by trade as much as Barbados does, but we prefer to look on it as a gentlemanly form of barter conducted in no great hurry, leaving us the rest of our time for beachcombing or whatever.' He paused. 'Tell me, do you really hope you're going to be able to bow out like Cinderella at the end of your time-span here?'

Staring into the misty distance, Lauren said, 'I must.'

'So you said—go back to England in search of a job. But has it to be England necessarily?'

'Why not? It's my home ground.' She smiled wryly. 'And an air ticket, economy class, will be about all I can afford. I've budgeted for England.'

'Quite. But other parts of the world need skilled technicians just as much—some, even more. For instance, we ourselves have to call on Barbados for a lot of things our small cottage hospital can't cope with. We have our people like you, of course, we couldn't carry on without them, but we have none to spare, and if you would consider staying and taking a therapy post, I assure you you'd get one. What about it?'

'Oh——' She turned quickly to him and away again. 'No. No, I couldn't.'

'You'd save yourself an economy fare to England!'

She had to meet his persuasive smile. 'Yes, but—No, I couldn't. That is, I couldn't—here. Anyway, why do you want to dissuade me from going back to England at the end of my fortnight?' she asked.

'Because,' he said, 'I think you haven't budgeted for a certain intangible expense.'

She frowned. 'Intangible? Such as?'

'The cost of emerging from your cocoon of pretended wealth. England in March, digs to find, the imperative need of a job. Here you'd let yourself down rather more lightly. Sun as a tonic, cheap food, two-by-four rented apartments going a'begging, no need for a wardrobe, for we live in shirts and slacks, and probably a job at the lift of a finger.' He laid a friendly hand over hers. 'Think about it, anyway. It was just an idea.'

'Thank you. I'm grateful. But I couldn't consider it here,' Lauren told him again.

'Why not? Once we land, which of our late companions is going to know or care that the late belle of our trip has decided to continue in her profession?'

'You warned me that, through your friendship with him, I might have to meet Dale Ransome,' she said unwillingly.

'Ah—Dale. Yes. And I promised to keep your secret from him?' Brian Gellhorn glanced at her shrewdly. 'It would matter, would it, if he especially learned it?'

'I'd rather he didn't.'

'Even if it only came out as a Cinderella trick you had played on us all for fun?'

She shook her head. 'He wouldn't see it as a joke. People hate to be fooled.'

'Surely only if the fooling catches them personally on the raw? And didn't you tell me that you and he weren't——?'

'Weren't nearly as close as anyone thought. In fact, weren't and aren't close at all,' she supplemented. 'It's just that—well, that I'd rather no one knew.'

'And that you be allowed to swan away into the sunset on your pink cloud of makebelieve?' He nodded. 'Very well, if that's the way you want it, I'll play it that way. For as long as you're at Le Marechal, I'll bar my doors to Dale and meet him somewhere else for a drink. Because you're coming to meet my Marthe, aren't you?'

'Please, I'd love to!'

'Good. I'll have her ring you, and we'll take you out. Pity we must steer clear of Dale's place, but there's plenty more of the island to see. Ah—' as the diesel throb deepened— 'we're moving in. Will the hotel meet you with a car?'

'I expect so.'

'And Marthe will be there for me, I hope. So if it's au revoir for now, remember it *is* only au revoir. Have you said goodbye to Dale?'

'Not yet. He doesn't seem to be around.'

'No. Not like Dale to have a sore head after a party, but perhaps last night's *was* a bit much,' Brian Gellhorn chuckled as he left her to go below.

CHAPTER FOUR

THE white ship stayed at the dockside for forty-eight hours, the loading of its cargo of bananas, avocadoes, aubergines and island cotton goods being a public spectacle for tourists and islanders alike. By the third morning it was gone, and with it the first half of Lauren's piece of extravaganza.

Le Marechal was luxury itself, with a magnificent view over the harbour and grounds extending to the edge of the lush green rain-forest and down, here and there, to hidden creeks opening out on to rock-strewn crescents of sand lapped by the lazy foam of the tideless sea.

The hotel's clientele was mainly American and Canadian, and almost every night was a gala affair. There was always dancing to a calypso steel band or the hotel orchestra after dinner, and somebody usually found an excuse to hold a party for a birthday or an anniversary—affairs which might end up at the swimming pool or in car trips into the mountains. On two or three nights the management gave their own drinks parties before dinner. But these Lauren managed to avoid attending, as they were held in the main bar and the adjoining lounge and she felt it possible that Dale might be there as someone's guest. She could not have borne to have witnesses to a chance meeting which they had bitterly promised each other shouldn't happen if either could help it.

Brian Gellhorn was as good as his word. On Lauren's second morning a soft, slightly accented voice called her on her bedside phone, identifying itself as belonging to Marthe Gellhorn, and inviting her to luncheon. Marthe would call for her in mid-morning and they would get to know each other over a drink, the voice promised.

Marthe matched her voice. She was small, gentle-mannered, a curly-headed brunette. At first Lauren was on her guard, not knowing what the doctor might have told his wife about herself, but as soon as she realised he had kept her secret, she relaxed to Marthe's friendly outgoing charm, and kept it herself.

It was while they were driving that Marthe revealed that she knew nothing of any tension between Dale and Lauren. Waving a hand towards a house just to be glimpsed in a group of trees higher up the hillside than the road, she said, 'That's Mont Michel, Dale Ransome's place. He came over with you, didn't he? Brian said so. Did you find him agreeable? He has charm, do you not think? He is a great friend of ours. When he is here we see him often. But I am afraid that while you are here—for a fortnight only, Brian says?—we may not be able to get him to meet you again, for he has told Brian he is going to be so busy that he can't keep any social dates for at least a month. It is nothing new, of course. Always, when he comes over, for a time we have to snatch at him when we can. And now he has the worry of his brother too. You have heard about Oliver Ransome from

Brian?'

Relieved that she hadn't had to agree or disagree as to Dale's 'charm', Lauren said 'Yes, your husband mentioned him, and another passenger told me about his accident and his trouble since.'

Marthe nodded. 'Yes, it would have had to be someone else. Brian won't talk about his patients, but I know he thinks Oliver has a—what is the English word?—ah, a block in his mind as well as the paralysis which will not let him walk—— But there!' she broke off with a guilty laugh, 'now it is I who am gossiping! Do not tell on me, will you?'

After a few more climbing hairpin bends the car turned in to the driveway of a timber-built house, surrounded by beds of flowering shrubs and shaded by towering flamboyants in full crimson blossom. When Brian arrived to join Lauren and Marthe, they lunched on the house verandah overlooking a dipping lawn, still steaming a little from an early morning rain. Before Brian came, Marthe had pointed out to Lauren a short cut footpath which led straight from their garden to Dale's land. But at lunch his name did not come up.

That was the first of several invitations Brian Gellhorn obtained for Lauren. She was bidden to picnic tours of the island, shown the whole cycle of banana culture, made a temporary member of the Yacht Club and a guest at a Government House garden-party. After years of needing to keep no record of dates more exciting than those with her dentist or her hairdresser, now her diary was excitingly full. Had she been all she appeared to be, she could have counted herself a social success. People seemed to like her, which pleased her—when she wasn't racked with guilt over her deception of them.

It was towards the end of her second week that Brian called for her to take her to lunch with them again. Marthe had had to keep an appointment in the town, but might or might not be home before them, Brian said.

She was there—and full of a triumph she was obviously panting to share.

'And whom do you think I captured on Jesuit Street?' she bubbled to Brian. 'Dale, no less! In his car, alone—nearly escaping me, but I stopped him. No, I told him. You have not been near us since you came over from England, and now I have caught you you will come to lunch. I will not take your No.'

Brian glanced quickly at Lauren. 'Did you tell him we had a guest?' he asked Marthe.

'No, I forgot. Forgive me, *chérie*.' She dimpled at Lauren. 'But it cannot matter—Dale and Lauren already know each other, do they not?'

'Oh yes. And so he's coming, is he?' Brian asked.

'He *promised*. He should not be long.' Marthe become the anxious hostess. 'I must go and tell Claribel we shall have a fourth for lunch,' she said, and went.

'Quite unforeseen, that. I'm sorry,' said Brian.

Lauren bit her lip. 'It can't be helped. It serves me right for being a coward. I shouldn't have involved you, and anyway, I shall be gone in a few days' time. As long as Dale needn't know about my play-acting until after then——?'

She made that a question. Brian replied, 'He shan't if I can help it, and Marthe can behave quite naturally. Have you booked your return flight yet?'

'I'm going to do it tomorrow.'

Marthe came back to say she had heard Dale's car taking the last corner, and all three stood there until he drove up the drive and got out.

He gave a hand to Brian, kissed Marthe—'You and your siren song! I should be with my bank manager,' he teased her, and acknowledged Lauren with a cool glance of neither surprise, nor the embarrassment she herself felt.

He said, 'So sorry to have missed you since we landed, but I hear by various sidewinds that you've been well fêted by our friends.'

She agreed, 'I have indeed, through introductions I never expected nor deserved. Everyone has been marvellously kind.'

'Mm—we're a gregarious lot, always ready to welcome those whom we recognise as our own kind from Home,' he said carelessly, conveying to Lauren the impression that he regarded her as nothing very special. Just a temporary interesting curiosity to the island's settlers and exiles from Europe and America, that was all.

As Brian poured rum punches and Marthe disappeared again, Dale asked, 'Are you going back by one of the Halcyon Ladys—probably *Cassia Lady*—on the next ship turnaround? Or are you going on—to Miami or New York perhaps?'

'No, I'm going home by air.'

'A very short trip. Hardly worth your trouble, surely?'

'Entirely worth my trouble. I've seen so much and made so many friends,' Lauren contradicted. 'It was only to be a holiday, after all.'

'A holiday from a life that's all holiday for a woman of leisure like you?'

'Is anyone's life all holiday? If so, it must be incredibly dull. And mine certainly isn't,' she parried.

'Ah yes—good works and the like—I forgot your interest in *them*,' he replied, and turned to talk to Brian who, Lauren felt, would have been puzzled and even embarrassed by the acidity of their exchange, since she had given him no reason to suppose her reluctance to meet Dale had any other cause than the keeping of her secret for her pride's sake.

He was telling Dale now that he had expected a call to Oliver Ransome since his own return from England. To which Dale replied, 'Yes, well—you know you're welcome to look in on him any time.'

'Socially or professionally?'

'Either. Both.'

'Then as I'd promised Lauren a sight of Mont Michel as one of our showpieces, may I bring her over for a social call before she leaves?'

Lauren deliberately did not look Dale's way as she awaited his reply. He told Brian easily, 'Of course, though you must make do with Oliver as host. I have to have a week in Barbados from to-morrow.'

'Oh, pity. Lauren plans to leave at the weekend.

But it's time I saw Oliver again, so I'll bring her over if she can spare the time. I'll ring Oliver beforehand, of course.'

'Yes, do that,' Dale agreed. He turned to Lauren. 'I'm sorry our chance meeting again has been so much a hail and farewell thing,' he said. 'But you'll be leaving your address in England with Brian and Marthe? So perhaps, the next time I'm over, I could call you and we might lunch or dine if you were free?'

And if you really meant that, or thought I would accept, you would have asked me for my address yourself, thought Lauren of as empty an invitation as she had ever had to murmur her conventional and equally empty thanks.

At the end of the meal to which Marthe called them then, she was to be surprised but relieved when Brian refused for her Dale's offer to drive her back to her hotel on his own way into the town. Brian said, 'No, we plan to keep her with us for the rest of the day. She has a date for dinner, but I'll get her back in time for that.'

They went to watch Dale drive off. Brian dismissed him with a casual 'See you, man', Marthe urged him, 'Do not make it so long next time, *chéri*!' and as she saw his car take the turn on to the road from the driveway, Lauren's heart bade farewell to a love she would never forget having known and didn't hope to know again. It wasn't there for her any more, but its brief hour had meant everything to her while it had lasted.

Before she left the Gellhorns she promised Marthe to see her again before she flew out, and

back at her hotel she was arranging to have
flowers and thanks sent to her several hostesses
when she was surprised to have a call from Brian.

'Dale is going down to Barbados on the evening
plane and I'd like to take you to Mont Michel
tomorrow, if that's all right with you,' he said.
'Oliver Ransome is expecting us, and I'll call for
you in the afternoon if I may. You can come?
Good.' He paused. 'And, Lauren——?'

'Yes?'

'Don't book your flight for Sunday until I've
seen you. O.K.?'

Under protest that if she left it later she might
not get a seat, she agreed. But when she asked him
why she should postpone her booking, he said,
'Sorry, not over the telephone,' and rang off.

That left her puzzling over his odd request until
he called for her the next day, and even then all he
told her was that if necessary he could pull some
strings to get her on to Sunday's flight, and did
not explain himself until he halted the car in a
natural layby on the road below Mont Michel.

Then, an arm crooked over the steering wheel,
he turned in his seat towards her.

'This will surprise you,' he said. 'But the truth is,
I'm hoping you'll make this call on Oliver Ransome as much of a professional visit as my own
will be.'

'*Professional?* What on earth do you mean?'

He laughed at her utter bewilderment. 'I
know—You think I've gone mad. But I mean it.
Oliver is a problem case who needs skills I haven't
got and you have, and not only physical therapy

but mental, with which I've a hunch your experience could help me to help him. I take it that Dale or Marthe or someone will have given you the layman's version of his case and its cause?'

Lauren shook her head. 'Dale didn't, but I heard from someone on board *Chaconia Lady*, that he was partially paralysed after a car crash, and Marthe has mentioned him. He's an orthopaedic case, and he isn't responding?'

'Nor will, I'm afraid, until we break down the mental block that's retarding him physically. He's young and strong, and there's no reason against his complete recovery, given regular therapy and exercise. But psychologically he's no more than a disc needle stuck in a groove of bitter disbelief that he *can* recover; even appearing careless of whether he does or not, to judge by his lack of co-operation with any treatment, psycho or physio. Let me be technical on his history for a few minutes, may I?'

He was, giving details for which Lauren, deeply interested, could find equally baffling parallels in her own experience. When Brian finished speaking, she said, 'It's not unusual, is it, for this kind of despair to set in when people, especially young ones, can't or won't believe there's still a future before them?'

'No, it's not,' he agreed. 'At first and sometimes for a long while, there's no break in their cloud, but once they co-operate in their therapy and begin to see progress, it's a different story. The difficulty here, though, is that so far Oliver has refused to work with anyone, and if he enjoys anything at all, he enjoys his own truculence. Sometimes I confess I could shake him and not least for his continuing diabolical rancour against Dale.'

'For Dale's having caused the accident to the car?' she questioned. 'But that's understandable. He may appear to enjoy his defeatism, but secretly he's ashamed of it, needs a scapegoat to blame for it, and chooses Dale.'

'Well, Dale *was* driving,' Brian reminded her.

'And in consequence Oliver should be in an orthopaedic hospital, having treatment, and you've asked me to look at him in the light of my therapy training, in order to confirm your diagnosis and the advice you'll give Dale to send him to one?'

Brian shifted in his seat, drummed his fingertips on the wheel. 'You've got it partly, but not exactly,' he said. 'Which brings us to my asking you to delay your leaving to plan. In short, I'm suggesting I give you Oliver's case for a course of therapy which nominally I shall direct, but which in practice I shall leave to you. What do you say?'

She stared at him. 'Say?' she echoed. 'What can I say but no?'

'You haven't seen the boy yet. Will you wait to refuse until you have?' he asked quietly.

'But you know I can't stay! You know why!'

'I know you'll be needing to take up your work almost as soon as you get to England, and I've argued why you shouldn't go, with less good reason than I have now. For here's a patient and work already laid on for you—work that I'm pretty convinced you have the character and the experience to do. And as soon as Dale gets back from Barbados——'

'But Dale Ransome is the reason why I can't stay!'

Brian frowned. 'Not principally, surely? I thought it was the running-out of your funds?'

'No—yes. Well, both,' she floundered, conscious of having given something away, though she was not sure what. She went on, 'That is, it's Dale at this stage. So far, I've escaped having to admit my piece of idiocy to anyone but you, and Dale is the last person with whom I've been at risk. I leave on Sunday; I don't have to see him again, and after that it won't matter.'

Brian sent her a shrewd glance. 'It's *so* imprtant to you that Dale shouldn't learn of your masquerade while you would have to meet face to face? I know I've aided and abetted you in it, but why should he think any the less of you than, for instance, I do, if he had to learn the truth?'

'He doesn't "think" anything particularly of me as it is.' Rallying, Lauren attempted a lie. 'No, it's just that if he or any of the others had found me out, I'd feel so guilty and a *fool*.'

Brian faced front again and switched on. 'My dear,' he said, 'if you aren't made to feel a fool at some time or other in your young life, you'll be lucky. But now we're going to see Dale's brother whom I think you could help if you would, and my offer to you of a watching brief still stands.'

She laid a hand on his arm. 'Please, Brian, no! There's no sense in my seeing him now.'

He removed her hand and placed it on her own knee. 'We've been invited and we're expected.

You're coming with me,' he said.

Mont Michel was all that Mr Cave's description had claimed for it. It was a long white house facing the sun and set in colour-bordered lawns where two West Indian gardeners were working. When Lauren admired both the expanse of gardens and the view, Brian said, 'Yes, Dale has the advantage of both height and access to the sea. Beyond that wicket'—he pointed—'there's a path which leads down to Orchid Point, an almost private cove where he swims.'

The annexe which Dale had given over to his brother's use was joined to the main house by a covered way. 'Typical of the staff quarters to a sugar plantation "great house" when no West Indian servants lived in,' said Brian. 'Most of them went home at night to shanty town, leaving only the major-domo and his wife on the place. Now Hector, Dale's houseman, sleeps in the main house, leaving the cottage to Oliver. And to his nurse, for as little time as he's tolerated one.'

The main door of the house stood open, giving on to a wide cool hall. Brian stepped inside and hallooed, 'Hector!', to be answered by a burly West Indian with an Afro-style haircut like a halo, and a broad smile.

'Ho, Doc Gellhorn,' he greeted Brian familiarly. 'Mister not home—gone down to Barbados, back in week.'

'Yes, I know. But we came to see Mister Oliver. He's expecting us, so may we go down?'

Hector looked doubtful. 'He in siesta, maybe. If so, he not pleased.'

'When he *is* pleased to see me, that'll be the day,' Brian countered, adding to Lauren, 'Come along. After all, he did invite us. I didn't twist his arm.'

At the door of the cottage he halloed again, and after a minute or two a young man propelled himself through from a back room in a wheelchair. His hatchet-thin face was a sallow edition of Dale's, his eyes were a cold slate, and the corners of his mouth drooped as no young mouth should. On Brian's introduction of Lauren, his faint smile was too much of a polite effort to be welcoming.

'Tea?' he asked.

'Good idea. I'll get it,' Brian offered, and disappeared, leaving Lauren alone with Oliver on purpose, she suspected. For something to say she launched on praise of the garden, only to be damped by Oliver's surly, 'Nothing to do with me.' She tried again. 'Brian says you can get down to the sea without leaving the grounds.'

'The sea?' His voice sharpened. 'You must be joking! How?'

She indicated his chair. 'Someone—your brother, his man—could push you down, couldn't they? And you could float, even if you can't swim—yet. It would do you good.'

The slate eyes narrowed on her. 'So that's why Doc brought you, to chant bromides like that at me? Do me a favour, will you? I've heard them all!'

'But haven't *listened* to any of them, have you?'

'Why should I? They don't do anything for me. Nothing and nobody can.'

'I'd like to take you up on that,' she retorted with spirit, but he brushed her aside.

'You're Brian and Marthe's friend, but Dale knows you too. Is that it?' he asked.

She calculated swiftly. It was possible that Oliver, a schoolboy then, had known of Dale's broken affair with a Lauren Kenyon. But he had shown no interest in Brian's introduction of her as Mrs Lauren Napier, and she decided to risk an evasion of the truth.

She said, 'Yes, I met your brother the last time *Chaconia Lady* came out from England. It was a marvellous voyage. But what did you mean—Is that it?'

'Well, isn't it?' he retorted. His glance was insolent. 'You aren't the first glamour bit he's brought to charm me into being civil. What about the one he's gone to Barbados to see—name of Mia Sumner, a synthetic blonde. Know her?'

'I don't know. I may have seen her. Someone met him when we docked at Barbados for the day,' said Lauren.

'Yes—well, you'll see more of her, as I've had to, more than enough. But she keeps on popping up, though she can't stand me, any more than I can stomach her. And now he's on the same tack with you? Introducing light and joy into my young life, by getting Doc to bring you to see me—Exhibit A in his cage.'

'As a matter of fact,' she corrected him, 'it was Brian who asked if he could bring me to show me the place. As far as Dale knew, meeting you would be incidental. Anyway, why should he want us to meet?'

'Probably to put the skids under me, by showing what I'm missing in the girl line—no?'

'*No.* That would be needlessly cruel while you're immobile. Your brother wouldn't do that, and in Doctor Gellhorn it would be unprofessional. You're baffling them both, but from what I've heard and after meeting you, do you know what I think?'

'Meaning, do I care what you think? Not in the slightest, but go ahead,' Oliver invited.

'Well, I think you're an exhibit in a cage largely by your choice; you're exploiting your inability to walk in order to annoy and worry—people.'

'Uh-huh? You suggest that I could get up this minute and *run* to, say, the front door? Come again, do!'

'Nothing of the sort. I'm only wondering whether, with the help of an arm, or a crutch or a stick, you couldn't *get* there somehow. I've been watching you. Under that rug you've been moving your legs, whether or not you can feel the gammy one——'

'Which I can't. But my word, aren't we getting clinical? Anyone would think you were one of those manipulating Sisters, physio—some-things——'

Oliver broke off as Brian came through with the tea. Wheeling himself out of Brian's way, he scoffed, 'You've got a right one here—ministering angel and pin-up cover-girl rolled into one! Anyway, oblige me, will you, by ringing Hector to bring me some tea in my room?'

Brian set down his tray. 'Nonsense, you don't have to bother Hector. If you aren't staying, I'll bring it to you myself.'

Oliver looked round over his shoulder. 'If you want me to throw it at you?' He propelled himself forward and reached to close a door behind him with a bang.

Brian did nothing about calling Hector. 'Well!' he said. 'That's something achieved. You've put him in a temper. Mostly up to now we've had only dumb insolence, not rage.'

Flushed, and as indignant for Brian as for herself, 'He's insufferable!' Lauren muttered.

Brian, pouring tea, questioned, 'But something of a challenge, eh?'

Knowing her flush had deepened and that Brian had noticed it, 'He would be, if I had to deal with him for long,' she admitted.

Brian passed her her cup, and drank from his own before he said quietly, 'Then what about it?'

She stared at him. 'Wh-what about what?'

'I think you've guessed. So will you agree now to postpone your flight home until the Sunday *after* next? Until after Dale is back, when we can talk?'

Lauren hadn't guessed, but she saw now how skilfully he had manoeuvred her to this point of challenge to her professional pride in her skill. He had played his hand low, but he had *meant* to interest and involve her in Oliver Ransome's case. He wanted to hand over the boy's treatment to her, and admiring him for his dedication, in any circumstances other than her own, she would gladly have agreed. As it was, she shook her head—'No.'

He nodded. 'Well, I hardly expected an eager Yes on the evidence. But could we perhaps kick it around in argument for a while? Go ahead—you begin.'

Much later, at her hotel, Lauren realised with what patient reasoning Brian had demolished all her objections.

She couldn't afford another week at Le Marechal. Could she not, if she saved the price of her return to England?

How could she live, where would she stay, if she even considered the impossible idea? Brian would rent for her a studio apartment and she would live on her pay, of course.

Her pay? She couldn't expect Dale to *pay* her! She didn't have to. Brian would be employing her as a physiotherapist, to 'special' with Oliver, but to be used on other cases if he saw fit; an arrangement which would have nothing financial to do with Dale at all.

Dale knew of her profession, but thought she was a rich woman who had retired from it on her marriage. He would never believe in any aboutturn in her future plans which could result in her practising again. He certainly wouldn't accept her for Oliver. Then if he didn't accept both the practitioner and the treatment Brian advised, Dale must find another doctor for both Oliver and himself, Brian claimed. And there was no way in which she could bring herself to confess to Brian why Dale would not be rejecting either an individual practitioner or a treatment. He would be rejecting *her*.

She had begun to feel trapped. Oliver himself would not accept her; he had taken dislike for her on sight. That was nothing new, said Brian. Any strange face seemed to put poison into his adrenalin, and he did his diabolic best to offend without appearing to lose his temper. But from the shop talks they had had on board *Chaconia Lady*, Brian had judged Lauren had the right approach to difficult patients, and he would back her to go at least some way with Oliver, if anyone could.

'I shan't get the chance,' she had said dully, and he had pounced on that.

'But you would like it?' he demanded.

'Things being different, I—yes, I think I would,' she had admitted.

'Then we have only Dale to persuade.'

'And Oliver!'

'Dale must threaten him with the blackmail of shipping him bodily to England if he refuses. It's Dale's house and Dale's enforced hospitality that he's using.'

Before they had parted Brian had had another suggestion to make. 'Wouldn't it all be a lot cosier and easier if you admitted to Dale that you're really just an ordinary working girl who's been kicking up her heels on a once-for-all binge?' he had asked.

But he had accepted her emphatic No to that; hadn't tried to persuade her.

All that week Lauren lived in dread of Dale's return, and not less in jealous speculation as to what the girl Mia Sumner was to him. Not that it mattered, she had to tell herself over and over. Brian had persuaded her, perhaps because she had half wanted to be persuaded. But he would never persuade Dale.

She expected that when Dale wanted to see her, Brian would bring him. But when he did come he came alone unannounced, and at a strangely chosen time of day.

She had a dinner date with an American fellow guest whom she did not particularly like and whose several persistent invitations she had refused, only accepting this one when, in her last days at the hotel, it could have no future commitments for her.

She was to meet her host in the main lounge of Le Marechal, and as he saw her and came over to her, she noticed Dale standing at the adjoining bar alone. He had seen her too and was level with her when she joined the other man.

She attempted an introduction—'Dale Ransome, Curtis Halgern', but her host stood aside, and Dale said, 'I want to see you.'

She nodded. 'Yes, but not now. I'm engaged.'

He glanced across at Curtis Halgern. 'Obviously. Then tomorrow?'

'Yes.'

'I'll be with you at twelve.'

'I—I'm supposed to be at a drinks party.'

'Skip it. We have to get this thing settled. 'Without waiting for her reply he nodded an apology to the other man and returned to the bar.

CHAPTER FIVE

DINNER with Curtis Halgern was not a success. He had very little conversation except double-meaning hints and jokes and anecdotes of exploits in which he was never the loser. As regards the menu, he had the annoying habit of overriding Lauren's choice and persuading her to dishes and drinks she did not want, and she was too preoccupied with her own problems to trouble to find some common interest they could talk about. The tiresome meal, lengthened by the leisurely intervals between the courses when people danced or were silenced by the steel band's clamour, seemed endless. Possibly as frustrated as she, her partner drank his way steadily through it, his jokes more risqué and his boasting more blatant as time strung out. And when it was over and Lauren planned her escape as soon as good manners allowed, he had other plans for the rest of the evening.

He tucked an intimate arm under hers. 'A few of the crowd are meeting us over at my place for coffee—*etcetera*,' he said with a smirk. 'They'll be there by now, so come along and we'll have a party.'

She hung back. His 'place', as she knew, was one of the rondavel-type chalets dotted about the hotel grounds for guests to rent instead of suites in the main building, and she had no taste for prolonging the evening with a party which might go on until dawn. 'No, I won't come, if you don't mind,' she said. 'Thank you so much for dining me, but they take so long to serve it that it's pretty late already, so I think I'll be turning in very soon.'

He ignored the hand she held out to him. His expression turned sullen. 'You can't stand me up just like that,' he protested. 'Nice fool I'll look, showing up alone when I'd promised the boys and girls I'd bring you along!'

'Oh no, I'm sure you can make my excuses for me,' she urged.

'But why should I? Dinner was nothing—it was just to get us in the mood for a good party—and now you want to back out!'

'You hadn't explained about there being any party.'

'I didn't know I had to. I thought you'd understand it wasn't "So long. Ta-ta. Thank you for having me," just as soon after dinner as you could get away. That's not playing fair.'

Lauren recoiled from the implication that she was expected to sing for her supper, but decided she had better humour him to a degree. 'Very well,' she agreed. 'I'll just come for coffee and then come away.'

'That means I shall have to see you back,' he grumbled.

'Nonsense. If I stayed until the end of what might be a very long party, I'd hope you *would* walk me back. But now, with everywhere lighted up and plenty of people about, surely I can manage a hundred or so yards of lawn without an escort?' she retorted.

As soon as she saw the darkened chalet intuition told her she had been tricked. Of course his friends might not yet have arrived, but still——! He had claimed to expect them to be there, but when she reminded him of this as he used his key on the door, he evaded with, 'Yes, well——' and opening the door, switched on a light to show the long lounge-cum-double bedroom which was standard in all the garden chalets.

There were no signs of preparation for any gathering of people. Only on a tray holding two cups and bowls of cream and sugar, the tiny working bulb of a coffee percolator glowed—the makings of a tête-à-tête, no more.

Lauren turned on him in the doorway. 'There's nobody here—you never meant there to be any party!' she accused him. 'You just——'

'That's right—wanted to be alone with you,' he confirmed with a grin. 'What's wrong with that?'

'Everything—since you had to lie to get me here. Pretending I was letting you down in front of your friends if I didn't come!'

'Look who's talking! You—pretending you didn't know we should be making a night of it,' he scoffed. 'Anyway, with all the easy girls there are around, why should I have bothered to ask you more than once, if there wasn't going to be anything in it for me?'

'In other words, I was going to have to earn my dinner?'

'Put like that—*are* going to earn it,' he retorted

nastily, taking her round the waist and attempting to push her inside.

She struggled. 'Let me go!' She fought him, but he pinioned her arms. 'I'll call for help. There are people about!'

'Call away. There's no one near enough to hear you, and if there were, they wouldn't interfere in an obvious clinch—like this——'

He was wrong there. As he caught her to him in a clumsy bear-hug, his mouth fumbling to find her lips as she turned her head this way and that to escape it, a figure stepped from the darkness into the fan of light from the doorway, and interfered between them by taking him by the shoulder and forcibly levering them apart. There was no mistaking the cold authority of Dale's voice as he demanded of the other man, 'This your pad?'

Halgern massaged his shoulder. 'What d'you think?' he blustered.

Dale said, 'I never think—I act. So if it's yours, get into it and go to bed—the only fit place for you until you're sober.'

'And who do you think you're telling to go to bed? And who's going?'

'*You* are—and alone.'

'Sez you! What about the girl-friend?'

Dale glanced across at Lauren. 'She may have asked for it, but you can leave her to me.'

'Why should I? Go find your own bit of stuff, feller. This one is frigid——'

Dale's reply to that was a resounding slap across the mouth which sent Halgern reeling and brought a shocked gasp from Lauren. Dale set Halgern back on his feet and gave him a push inside the door. 'Good night to you,' he said. 'Where's your key? Then lock yourself in and put down your night-catch in case I come back to pick another quarrel.' He took Lauren firmly by the elbow and matched his pace to her slower, high-heeled progress across the lawns to the main building. His very silence until they reached it was a judgment of her, and shaken and humiliated, she longed for him to accuse her, so that she could clamour in her defence that she hadn't 'asked for it', that she had been tricked.

In the foyer he asked her what was her room number, fetched her key from the desk and went up in the lift with her to her floor. At the door to her room he remarked, 'I must say, you appear to be a magnet for less desirables—for instance, stubborn and amorous drunks like the one you collected tonight.'

'I didn't know,' she protested. 'And that's unfair. I haven't been bothered by any other drunk since I——'

She had meant to say, 'since I came', but he cut in and supplied for her—'since your last night on board the *Lady*—hm? You had to deal with one then? Or so you claimed.'

She flushed at the reminder. 'I was wrong. I realised afterwards that you hadn't been drinking,' she admitted.

'Wrong twice over. I had, and continued to do so after I left you. But thanks for the apology, if that's what it was meant to be. As for tonight, how come you fell for that fellow's ploy, whatever it was?'

'He told me he'd laid on a party for me, and that I'd be letting him down, if I didn't go.'

'About as corny a line as wanting you to see his etchings. Don't you know that, to his type, a woman travelling alone is a scalp he can't bear to pass up? Couldn't you afford to bring along some young thing disguised as a social secretary, to ward off the more obvious wolves?'

'I *wanted* to travel alone,' she muttered.

'But after only three weeks or so, tired of it enough to toy with this crazy idea of Brian's to put you back to work you don't need and which Oliver will do his best to prevent your doing?'

'If I thought I hadn't a chance with him, I wouldn't have discussed my trying with Brian.'

'When my non-co-operative brother has seen off every well-meant offer of help and therapy to date?'

'Because he is enjoying his grudge against life too much to want to get well just yet.'

'Meaning it's mental as much as physical? Well, Brian knows that, but—— Meaning too his grudge against me? You'll have heard the story?'

She nodded Yes. 'But I've only said I'd try.'

'For how long?'

'I'd like to say, for as long as it takes to get anywhere with him. He needs physical action—exercises and so on—as well as understanding, and I may not be able to administer either. But I'd like to try.'

Dale commented, 'Ever the lame dog appeal. I must say you cut true to pattern all through.'

Her shoulders sagged with weariness and frustration at his detachment. 'Yes, perhaps, and you've never had any sympathy with my lame dog priorities—my concern for Lucille, my marrying Steven for pity. I believe you would even be glad in a twisted way if Oliver defeated me too,' she accused him.

' "Too"?' he echoed. 'Then you did come to rue the day over Lucille and Steven Napier?'

She had—bitterly—for love and loss of him. But if to admit it meant a petty triumph for him, she would not. She said, 'I followed my conscience over both of them, and I hope I'd do the same again. Your brother's case is different. It would be a challenge to whatever skill I may have, and if I could do anything for him, it would justify Brian's belief in me, and I value that.' She longed to add that his own belief in her mattered over all, but that was too much to ask of her fate.

He said, 'Forgive me if to me it looks like quixotry for quixotry's sake, won't you? But I'll bring Brian along to talk it out in the morning.'

'Thank you.' She added, 'Thank you too for—tonight.'

'The knight-errant bit?'

'Yes. How did you happen still to be here?'

'I'd skipped dinner at home and stayed at the bar, giving you time to learn your lesson.'

Lauren worked that out. 'You thought I was asking for trouble by dining with that man? How did you guess?'

'From the dirty sniggers at the bar when you met him and went with him into the dining-room.'

She flushed with shame. 'They knew him for what he is?'

'Only too well, apparently. Which made the knight-errantry rather necessary, I thought. Your wealth has brought you a lot of glamour and sophistication, but I'd say you rate pretty low in your judgment of men, my dear.'

At any other time she might have been driven to retort, 'Don't patronise me!' or 'You don't know anything *about* my judgment of men.' But, bathed in the glow of hearing Dale had cared enough to rescue her from Halgern, she wanted him to confirm it.

'Then you didn't just happen by? You were enough concerned to follow us up?' she questioned.

'Knowing what my own reactions might have been, having got you so far—either willing or incredibly gullible—yes.'

It wasn't the answer she wanted. 'I don't think you would have forced me,' she argued, hopeful that he wouldn't remind her again of that last night on board.

But he did. 'You're as short on memory as you are on know-how about how our sex reacts under the pressure of lust or frustration especially with a desirable female. I'm a man like any other, and you shouldn't make any mistake that we're not all animal opportunists, every one.'

Disappointed to her core, she said nothing. Dale opened her door for her and handed her the key. 'You know, however rich you are, you would probably have been wise to stick to do-goodery as your main role,' was his parting comment as he left her.

Dale having implied overnight that she was a failure as a butterfly and should have been content with the safe backwaters of her professsion, Lauren was not surprised that, at their meeting the next morning, he made few difficulties over her proposed treatment of Oliver.

The meeting became a mere discussion of ways and means, with Dale wanting first to know where she proposed to live while she was treating Oliver.

'I'd thought of taking for her one of those one-room villas on the edge of town, as she would prefer that to staying on here,' said Brian.

'No. Those places are too isolated, and until they build more of them, too scattered. She's not to live alone there. I'd like her to stay at Mont Michel while she's dealing with Oliver. She can have the garden room overlooking the cottage, and that will save her any problem of to-and-fro travel,' Dale ruled.

'Oh!' Brian turned to Lauren. 'How do you feel about that?'

She knew he must have expected her to veto it, but since, however rashly, she had invited further contact with Dale, she accepted his ultimatum. 'If you think that's the best arrangement,' she told him.

'Good. Hector and Melie, my man and his wife, will see that you have everything you want. When may we expect you?' he asked.

'I'm booking out from here on Sunday.'

'Then I'll send the car for you. Ring to tell me when.'

'Thank you.' Supposing that was all they need discuss, she stood up. But Dale asked abruptly, 'As a matter of interest, how do you propose to approach Oliver's case in the first place? Still as Brian's friend, breaking it to him only gently that your interest in him is professional? Or do you plunge in straight away in a white coat with a manual on remedial exercises under your arm? That is, if you haven't forgotten how to use the professional touch by now?'

Even at so formal an interview as this, he couldn't resist the temptation to bait her! 'How do *you* advise me to introduce myself?' she asked Brian.

Brian mused, 'Mm—tricky. I think I must leave you to play it by ear, bearing in mind that, from Oliver's parting shots, he already suspects you of clinical designs on him, however socially interested you appear to be at first.'

'And as he has to know I'm staying in the house, he'll naturally conclude it's for some purpose,' she agreed. From the corner of her eye she caught Dale's faint smile at that. 'Not that it's unusual for women friends to stay at my invitation without any purpose other than that I want them there,' he murmured, adding in parenthesis to Brian, 'Mia is coming up shortly for a few days,' before continuing, 'And none of them, as far as I know, have minded being chaperoned by Hector and Melie in our otherwise bachelor establishment. But I agree, and I shall warn Oliver beforehand that Lauren is there for the reason she *is* there. It might take the heat off his reception of her if I can tell him she did go to see him under false colours the other day.'

Brian nodded approval. 'Good thinking. Any man likes to be proved right.' He smiled at Lauren. 'And so, the ground prepared for you, you'll know just where you stand, and can take it from there, can't you?'

Dale's dispassionate gaze was considering Lauren—her besandalled feet and slim brown legs, her ivory thigh-length tennis dress with its trim of broderie anglaise and the flare of the white ribbon bow tying up her hair in readiness for a date on the courts in a few minutes' time. 'And of course we can rely on you to play your part—manner, dress, the lot, with all the flair we've come to expect of you?' he insinuated, and without looking for a reply, invited Brian for a drink.

Brian chuckled, 'I'll back her to do it so thoroughly that we shall hardly recognise her as anything *but* a physiotherapist on duty.'

And you *bet* I'll see that Dale comes to accept me for what I am—"manner, dress, the lot"—was Lauren's unspoken resolve as they parted.

It was Hector who called for her when she left Le Marechal. At Mont Michel she had made the acquaintance of Melie, a buxom lady, all smiles and welcoming noises, had been shown her room and had lunched alone. Hector told her Oliver had chosen to lunch in his cottage, and Dale did not appear.

After lunch she gave Oliver time for his siesta and then screwed her courage to going down to see him. She wore a plain linen suit, taking with her neither the white coat nor the exercise manual of Dale's sarcastic suggestion, but on impulse, tucking under her arm a rolled satchel containing coloured wools and a half-finished canvas of petit-point embroidery.

She found Oliver lying on a sunlounger on his porch. His greeting to her was a nod and a studiedly bored closing of his book, keeping his thumb between the pages. Her greeting to him was an outstretched hand, which he ignored, waving instead to a nearby chair. 'So sorry I can't get it for you,' he sneered.

Lauren fetched it herself and sat down, facing him. 'I'm not welcome, and no wonder,' she said. 'We didn't exactly get off on the right foot with each other the last time, did we?'

'Your fault. And you don't imagine you and Doc fooled me for a second? Either you were another of Dale's floosies, all tea and sympathy, or you were a spy, sent to report on me with a view to future action, and it didn't need Dale to admit I was right. So—when do we begin?' He narrowed his glance on the satchel now in her lap. 'What's that thing? Your nurse's cap and apron? Or a Mickey Mouse mask to keep the patient amused?'

She unrolled the canvas, showed him what it was and began to thread a needle. 'We don't begin until you're willing,' she told him. 'And as I thought you might not be, and I like to use my hands, I brought it along to work at until you are.'

She nodded at his book. 'Read if you want to. I don't mind.'

Oliver's cold eyes stared. Then he opened his book, appearing to read, though with no more concentration, Lauren guessed, than she was bringing to her needlework. Battle was joined; they both knew it, and it was a toss-up as to who gave in first.

He did. 'This is idiotic,' he declared. 'You aren't earning your keep and I'm as bored as all get out. So let's get cracking, may we? Where do you want to prod first? Or shall I do a knees bend—knees stretch while we both hum Nuts In May?'

She put aside the canvas. 'Neither. I'd rather we talked,' she said.

'We talked the other day, and you were filthily rude.'

She laughed. 'Quits. So were you.'

'You accused me of malingering—told me I could walk if I wanted to!'

'Not if you wanted to, for I'm sure you do.'

'What makes you think so?'

'Because at your age and with all your future going for you, you'd be a fool if you didn't *want* to. No, what I thought I said was that for some stubborn quirk of your own, you didn't seem willing to help yourself even halfway. Or to admit that other people—just possibly—might be able to help you the other half. That anyone would expect you to get up and walk, just like that, is absurd. For one thing, you've been immobile for so long that your muscles alone wouldn't take it—but I could help with that. I don't know what the quirk is, and

I don't suppose you'll tell me, even if you know yourself, and you may not. But either you snap out of cherishing the quirk, or you begin by trying the physical things—the massage, the over-and-over boring routines, even stepping over a rope and pretending you're skipping—Doesn't matter which comes first. But as I see it, it could be as simple as that.'

Lauren drew a long breath, feeling spent with a persuasion she had little hope would have any effect. But she had had to try it, and without appealing to his will and his reason, they would get nowhere. They had to work as a team.

Oliver said, 'For "quirk" read "cussedness"? O.K., I'm cussed for the sake of it. Is that what you're saying?'

'Nothing of the sort. I think you're being as obstructive as you are because, for all I know, you may have very good cause.'

'H'm—handsome of you to admit I might have! So tell me, what would be *your* idea of a "good cause"?'

'Well,' she hesitated,' supposing you were deeply afraid? So afraid of never being as whole as you were before your accident that you wouldn't try physical treatment, lest the result should fall short of our promises to you?'

He appeared to consider that—which was something. But he finally shook his head. 'That would be pretty dumb of me,' he said. 'How do *I* know what the medics could or couldn't do for me?'

'I agree. Well then, at a venture—you might

have a grievance against something or someone, which you felt was justified and which you
could register where it would hurt only by digging in your heels and telling the world "No
way"?'

'No way—what?'

'No way would you play along with any plans
for you while the grievance rankled. Treatment
here, which could do a lot. Going back to England
to see top-rank consultants, which would be even
better——'

'Huh!' There was no mirth in Oliver's short
laugh. 'Don't pretend you thought *that* one up for
yourself!' he accused. 'You've been listening to the
gossips, and for once the gossips are right. It's all
over town, no doubt—"It was *Dale* Ransome who
was driving the car when they ran out of road—
Dale Ransome, the Halcyon King, who escapes
without a scratch while his young brother got
broken up. You'd think he'd feel some guilt over
that"—and so on and so on. You'll have heard
that, and it's true. And in my shoes, left as I am,
wouldn't *you* want to take it out in cussedness all
round?'

Lauren said quietly, 'I'd want to, yes. But——'

'—But you'd be too forgiving, too noble-
minded, eh? Which I'm not.'

'Nor should I be. But I hope I'd see the idiotic
futility of making a meal of blame for an accident
that had happened and was over. They must be
happening every day on these roads, and aren't
necessarily anyone's fault.'

'This one was.'

She ignored that to go on, 'And I think—
though this I couldn't be sure of—though you've
been rather enjoying your notoriety as your
brother's innocent victim, sooner or later you're
going to be bored by seeing everyone else moving
around normally, and you'll begin to see the sense
of co-operating.'

'You think I shall, do you? Well, don't hold
your breath while you're waiting.'

'I won't,' she said more patiently than she felt. 'I
told you I couldn't be sure.'

She hadn't his attention as she finished speaking. He was looking beyond her, and turning, she
saw Dale standing not far behind her chair.

'I'm sorry, I had to leave Hector to install you,'
he said, and to Oliver, 'Do you want him to bring
you up to the house for dinner?'

Oliver turned his chair to the open door behind
him. 'I don't know. You can send him down, and
I'll see.' He wheeled himself away.

Dale said, 'Melie is putting tea on the terrace for
us. Will you come?' and then, 'I thought Brian
would have been with you to get things moving.
But you introduced yourself?'

'Yes. I asked Dr—Doctor Gellhorn to give me a
free hand, and he agreed I should go ahead as I
thought best.'

Dale frowned. 'Doctor Gellhorn?' he questioned. 'Why the sudden formality, pray?'

Longing to remind him of "dress, manner, the
lot", Lauren said, 'I'm merely being correct. He's
employing me on your brother's case. He's paying
my salary.'

'And by the same token, you and I are "Mrs Napier" and "Mr Ransome", I suppose? Well, you can forget it, and the Doctor Gellhorn bit too.'

She agreed, 'Very well—off duty. But I'd prefer to be Mrs Napier in front of Oliver.'

'Why?'

'Because it puts me in my place, as the professional employee I am. He's still resenting the way I was first introduced to him—as a friend of yours, and to pay us out for that he feels he has to slap me down. Whereas my being Mrs Napier to you and Brian, instead of an intimate, puts me among the workers where I belong, and enough beneath him to save him the trouble of snubbing me, he'll consider. Or I hope he will,' she added wryly. 'It'll be one hurdle taken.'

'But he's intent on snubbing you now?'

'He's doing his best. You could say we're sparring verbally, with no holds barred, but no blood to speak of being drawn as yet.'

They had reached the terrace where a table was laid and a brass kettle was steaming on a spirit-lamp stand. Dale drew out a chair for her and took charge of the tea-tray himself. Making the tea and stirring it, he said,

'That's the sum total of your first session, then? A wary conversation piece? Let's see—did Brian engage you as a physiotherapist for Oliver, or a trick-cyclist—I forget?'

He may have intended a joke, but coming from him, Lauren took it hardly. Her hand shook a little as she took the cup he passed to her. She said,

'Brian could tell you that in cases like your brother's, psychiatry has to go hand in hand with the physical, remedial stuff; has to go before it and break down the opposition first, very often. And that's the way Brian agreed I should approach it—by trying for the mental core of Oliver's obstructive attitude, and it could take time finding it.'

Dale was watching the swirl of the tea in his cup. 'Though weren't you on the track of a possible cause when I came by just now?' he asked. 'Weren't you in earnest discussion of the case against the guilty party, with you agreeing that in his place you would have reacted as he has done?'

Lauren thought back to Dale's appearance on Oliver's porch. 'You stood there and heard us?'

'At first behind the croton hedge before I showed myself. I heard you leading him into the suggestion of his having a grudge against me which hadn't been resolved; him, quoting the local judgment of me very accurately, and you, as I've said, admitting you found his attitude justified.' He shrugged. 'In fact, the eavesdropper's reward.'

She nodded. 'Except that you weren't listening very carefully, if you didn't hear me say that, though I'd feel the same bitter resentment, I'd have more sense than to let it eat me to the point where it was becoming my own enemy—you didn't hear that?'

'I must have been rounding the croton hedge. And has that argument got you anywhere?'

'I don't know. You appeared just then.'

'So no break-through yet?'

'Considering how long he's stood out, it would

be remarkable if there were, and until he's willing I can't force any regular physical treatment on him,' Lauren told him. 'But he does need to get those lazy muscles moving, and there's a way in which your man could help in that, if you would let him.'

'Hector? How?'

'Well, when I mentioned to Oliver the other day that he might try swimming, he only scoffed that he couldn't, not that he wouldn't. And as there's no reason why he shouldn't at least float, given support, I've been thinking that if Hector could take him down to your creek in his chair, he might agree to go.'

'The snag about that being that the adult West Indian is a notoriously reluctant swimmer, so that Hector wouldn't fill the bill,' said Dale.

'Oh! Then that's out. I thought——'

'Not necessarily,' he cut in. 'If it would do him any good, *I* could push him down to the Point and do any life-saver stuff that was wanted.'

Lauren hesitated. 'That would be marvellous,' she said, though aware her tone lacked conviction.

She saw Dale's brows go up. 'Offer accepted con enthusiastic brio?' he hinted sarcastically. 'Take it or leave it, as you please.'

'I'll take it, of course,' she assured him quickly. 'Thank you. It was just that I'm wondering whether Oliver will.'

'Coming from me, you mean?'

She nodded reluctantly. 'Coming from you.'

'He'll take it—or else.' He stood up as he saw she was rising from the table. They faced each other across it. 'You aren't going to bludgeon him,' Lauren said heatedly.

'I'd have thought it was your office to see I don't have to,' he retorted. 'When do I report for duty?'

'Give me time to suggest it to him. The day after tomorrow, perhaps?'

'I have to collect Miss Sumner at the airport in the afternoon. I think you met her briefly at Barbados? But I shall be free in the morning,' Dale offered.

'Thank you.' Lauren looked back on her way into the house. 'I shall need to be there, you know,' she told him.

'But of course. What could be more exciting than a triangular bathing party; every corner with different reasons for being at odds with the other two?' he mocked with a pseudo-gallantry which enraged her.

CHAPTER SIX

OLIVER'S reaction was negative but not actively hostile.

'It's a fool idea. It won't do any good. I'll go if I feel like it, but if I don't want to bother, you can forget it,' was his grudging verdict when Lauren suggested the swim.

'I hope you'll decide to come,' she told him. 'You say you don't sleep well, so if the effort only tires you out it will be something. I suppose you'll change up here and go down in your trunks?'

'Dale swims in the buff, and so did I. There's a rock or two and some piled driftwood where you can strip off and towel down. Are you coming too?' he asked.

'Oh yes. I want to see how you manage.'

'Then I suppose we'll have to keep our trunks on. What a bore!' he yawned.

Lauren changed in her room into a short towelling robe over her suit and waited for Dale on the terrace. On the way down to the cottage she asked him if there were any hazards at the Point.

'The water's like a millpond. The only nuisance is the sandflies which the holiday brochures take care not to mention.'

'Yes, I was warned at Le Marechal about them, but I've not been troubled by them yet.'

'You will be. Brought any repellent with you

today?'

'Yes, in my bag.' She patted her straw shoulder satchel.

'Good. Use it if you're going to sit about,' Dale ordered.

Oliver was in his wheelchair with a towel round his bare shoulders, pale and flaccid, in contrast with Dale's golden-tanned torso which Lauren ached to touch, to caress ... as she would have longed to smooth the pelt of a fine wild animal, known to be dangerous and so forbidden to her.

At the shore, a curve of white sand bordered by wind-slanted palms, and the little bay itself sheltered from the north by a long finger of rock, Dale got as near to the surf-line as he could take the chair, and Lauren knelt on the sand to shed her robe. Oliver was being difficult about leaving the chair, grunting with effort and ignoring Dale's efforts to help him. At last Dale picked him up bodily with consummate ease and waded far enough into the sea to enable Oliver to float and himself to tread water, supporting him with a hand under his head.

Lauren paddled, watching for some sign that Oliver was something more than a cradled, inert body, and after some time was gratified to see him kick out with his able leg, turn over and begin to use that leg and one arm in a splashing and slapping sidestroke, independent of Dale. He was swimming in a fashion! Her heart lifted. Surely he would be as encouraged by the small achievement as she was, and Dale mightn't grudge her an appreciative word for having urged or shamed Oliver into his first compliance?

After a few strokes Oliver turned to float again, spouting like a whale. Dale continued to swim beside him, and Lauren went out to them, using a leisurely crawl.

Oliver sputtered, 'How was that?' as if he cared about being praised.

'I wasn't surprised; I knew you could,' she told him, and Dale said obliquely,

'I wonder Brian didn't suggest this before,' though he must know, Lauren thought, that Brian probably had, only to have the idea shot down by Oliver.

She signalled to Dale to swim away. 'Let me——' she said, taking his place at Oliver's side.

'You can't——'

'Nonsense, of course I can. Look, he's not even needing my hand.'

'He could panic and grab you.'

'Let him grab.' She turned a confident face to Dale's. 'Don't you know that swimming therapy and, if need be, lifesaving is a major thing in physiotherapy training?' she asked.

He did, she knew. For in the old days when he had cared for her, he had wanted to hear every detail of her life. She went on, 'When you can't come with him, I must, if you would ask Hector to wheel him down and back. I'd like him to swim two or three times a week.' As soon as she spoke she realised her words implied she was thinking of her job in terms of at least weeks, and wished Dale would give some indication of his own ideas about it. But all he said was, 'I'll see Hector and tell him'—accepting her will for the first time without argument.

Oliver managed a few more strokes under her guidance, then they turned for the shore and Dale went back to swim far out while Lauren sat on the sands by Oliver's chair.

It took him to question her stay for the length of time she had implied. 'Who says I'm going to be at the receiving end of your theories and practices for as long as "weeks"?' he asked, truculent as ever.

'You'll do the saying, I hope,' she told him.

'I had no say in bringing you here!'

'But there'll be no point in my staying if you don't play along,' Lauren pointed out.

He threw her a calculating glance. 'Sure the attraction isn't big brother Dale, and I'm just a pawn in your play for him? Anyway, I don't mind swimming, but what's the rest of the drill? I may as well hear the worst.'

Encouraged, she said, 'Well, primarily there's your will to get well and to want more for yourself beyond just walking again without help. Then——'

'More? Such as what?'

'Well, the confidence that you can drive a car again, ride a horse, play games——'

'And have the girls queueing up, I suppose?' he sneered.

Lauren laughed. 'If you cared to exert yourself to attract them *now*, you'd probably find them beating a path to your door. There's a bit of Florence Nightingale in all of us. As for the drill, as you call it, there ought to be massage——'

'Yes, we know all about *massage*, don't we?' he hinted darkly.

'Don't be cheap,' she snapped. 'It'll be hard physical work for me, and no fun for you. And exercises for the rest of your body—arms and shoulders and torso, because all your muscles will have atrophied while you've been sitting around. But when your thigh and gammy leg hurt instead of being numb, that'll be the day.'

'And all this will take weeks?'

She dared not tell him it could take much longer. 'It could probably be much quicker if you'd go back to England for the very latest in electro-therapy,' she told him.

'And I am not—repeat not—going back to England.'

'Why not?'

'Because it would suit Dale to be rid of me.'

'I see.' It was all she could trust herself to say.

'You don't, but no matter.' Oliver stared out to sea. 'Where has he got to? I've *had* this, I want to go back,' he grumbled.

So, for a different reason, did Lauren. On looking in her satchel she had found that she had not, after all, brought the insect-repellent, and she was being continually attacked by the hover of sand-flies around them. Their bites must have been full of venom, for they raised disfiguring yellow blisters almost at once and her neck and face and bare back were massed with them. When Dale swam back at last and came up the beach there was no hiding them from him.

'I thought you said you'd brought some protection?' he said.

'I'd meant to, but didn't. Aren't they a sight?' For some reason she had begun to shiver.

'You'll get inured to them. We natives do. It's too late for repellent, but I have something for them when we get back to the house. Go on up. I'll park Oliver and follow you. Wait on the terrace for me.'

Not long behind her, he went through into the house, returning with a tube of gel for which she held out her hand. 'How do I use it?' she asked.

Dale was squeezing some on to his own fingertips. Jerking an elbow at her robe, 'Take that thing off; I'll do your back which you can't reach,' he ordered. 'It's going to sting.'

It did, and she flinched. But his touch was infinitely gentle, reminding her poignantly of the magical summer of their meeting when they had shared their suntan lotion and had applied it in turn. She wondered if he were remembering too. But he gave no sign that his task was anything more than a clinical necessity.

He watched her do her arms and face. 'Feeling all right?' he enquired.

'Yes.' Her teeth chattered slightly. 'Why?'

'Because they've been known to trigger off an allergy—set up a fever. You'd better go to your room. Don't dress again; get into bed and I'll call Brian to have a look at you.'

Lauren protested against that, but Dale picked up her robe and went with her to her room, on the way telling Melie to serve her lunch to her there. He would see her again in the evening after collecting Mia Sumner from the airport, he told her.

She was grateful for the touch of cool sheets on her burning skin. She accepted from Melie only some crispbreads and milk and fell into a feverish doze from which she roused to find Brian at her bedside.

He scolded her mildly, took her temperature, gave her an injection and promised her the inflamed pustules would have subsided after twenty-four hours in bed. She was suffering a very mild form of tropical fever, but it would immunise her. The pestiferous little so-and-so's preferred virgin skin.

He stayed to ask about Oliver.

'Difficult,' she grimaced. 'But he will swim, I think.'

'Accepting Dale as transport and crutch? That's something.'

'When Dale is free. Otherwise he'll have to tolerate me and Hector. I can see him again tomorrow?' she asked anxiously.

'If your temperature is down in the morning. Dale shall report on you and ring me. You feel you may have gained a foothold with Oliver and you don't want to lose it?'

'*If* I've gained one——!'

Under the influence of the injection Lauren slept again, and felt better when she woke. It was six o'clock. Dale had said he would see her in the evening, and she would *not* see him from her bed. She got up, put on the expensive négligé she had bought for her trip, and, refraining from facing her pockmarked image in the mirror, was brushing her

hair when there were voices outside her room—
Dale's and the light, bored tones she had last
heard on the deck of *Chaconia Lady* on the night
when Dale had been ready with his verbal whip for
her, and later with an assault which had fired her
body's desire for him at the same time as it had
humiliated her will.

There was a knock, and he and Mia Sumner
came in, the girl's white-blonde hair now loose
upon her shoulders, her tall figure in a sleeveless
sheath of brilliant jewel colours, a white duster-
coat careless over one arm. Her other hand was in
Dale's.

Dale introduced Lauren to her. Her glance, as
Lauren had known it would, went pityingly to
Lauren's ravaged face. 'My *dear*,' she exclaimed,
'you *must* be accident-prone! Because we have met,
haven't we—for a second? You remember, Dale?
At Barbados, when Mrs Napier had been trying
conclusions with the natives or something which
had left her looking a *wreck*? You poor, poor
thing!' she addressed Lauren again. 'Why didn't
somebody warn you? Or didn't you listen? *We*
never suffer, of course, but all our nastier creatures
seem to home in on you unfortunate tourists.'

Lauren resented the implication that tourists
were somehow of a lesser breed than the islanders.
She said, 'I was warned, and I did listen. I was
forgetful, that was all, and I'm paying for it. Brian
says I can be about tomorrow, but that I'm to stay
here tonight,' she added to Dale.

Dale said, 'That's what I thought he would tell
you.'

'I'd meant to see Oliver again this afternoon. I'm sorry,' she apologised.

'Not that he's likely to miss you, is he? Dale says you're finding getting next to him is like treading on broken glass, and really one can't think why you *bother*?' Mia Sumner questioned, and was answered by Dale's dry comment,

'You wouldn't—not being on 'the same dedicated beam as Brian Gellhorn and Lauren here, both of whom would not only walk on broken glass, but give the impression they would willingly swallow splinters of the stuff for the sake of their art.'

Lauren frowned at the cynicism, and Mia tittered, 'Oh dear, that makes the rest of us sound impossibly frivol-minded!'

'Not at all. Just—human,' he corrected.

She brightened, as at a deserved compliment. 'You do make a girl feel good, Dale,' she purred, adding to Lauren as she turned towards the door, 'That's *his* special art, as you'll find if you're ever at the receiving end of it!' She went ahead of Dale after dropping her coat over his arm, leaving Lauren to wonder whether she had to work at subtly poisonous remarks or whether they came naturally. And they were to be house companions for as long as Mia's visit lasted!

Lauren's imagination followed her and Dale through the rest of the evening. After her flight from Barbados Mia would change and they would have a drink together. Mélie, bringing Lauren's own modest supper of buttered eggs and rice, said they were not going out, so they would dine tête-à-tête, Oliver having declined to be present. Afterwards they would probably take their coffee on the terrace, and talk, and skirt the fringes of their intimacy, promising themselves who-knew-what of the night hours when the house would be asleep and its freedoms to meet and make love until dawn all theirs . . .

In the morning Mia would be vivaciously alive, and Dale aggressively male and fulfilled, while she herself, blotched like a victim of plague, would appear like an untouchable. Jealousy of Mia took her by the throat, seeming to threaten to choke her.

Later, close to midnight, the air turned intolerably humid and hot. Getting out of bed to switch on the air-conditioning, she drew back the curtains of her window which looked out over the garden towards Oliver's cottage. Storm clouds were chasing the moon, overtaking it and blotting it out, then racing on. When it emerged, by its light she could see movement out there—two people strolling very slowly, very close. As Lauren watched, the woman—Mia, who else?—stopped, took the man's hands, set them upon her shoulders, turned her face up to his, inviting his kiss.

After a moment they turned back to the house, as if the kiss had confirmed some unspoken agreement between them. Forgetting her errand, Lauren dropped the curtain and tumbled back to bed. Of course she had known that was how it was. This wasn't her jaundiced imagination. This was fact.

It was just as well that Oliver's trips to the shore

were not to be dependent upon Dale's help, for Mia monopolised as much of Dale's company as she could, driving out with him on business or visits to friends, of whom she seemed to have as many as he on the island. They swam together down at the Point, or she swam alone, but never when Oliver was there.

Their hostility was common to both of them, their aloofness as complete as circumstances would allow. At first Lauren wondered whether Oliver's animosity towards Mia could be a kind of frustrated attraction, turned to resentment of Mia's vivacious beauty. That is, he might hate Mia for a feminine appeal to which his own disability could not respond, just as probably he was jealous of Dale's virility compared to his. But that did not explain Mia's equal antipathy for him, nor her purposed avoidance of him, about which there was something almost wary.

Wary of Oliver? Why should she be? Or, for that matter, he of her? All the same, it seemed to Lauren that two thieves who had fallen out could hardly have been at worse odds. Not that it was likely, she thought, they could ever have been close enough to share the kind of dark secret which people like thieves needed to keep. As a problem, she gave it best, but as a fact their enmity served her well.

For inevitably her work with Oliver ranged her on his side, making her task easier by reason of his needing an ally against Mia. Unashamedly she exploited that, with the result that, far sooner than she had expected, he was showing a faint interest in what she was trying to do for him.

Boredly, he would listen while she described the need for some exercise she prescribed; equally noncommittal, he might agree to try it—or not, according to his mood. But these she came to be able to read, and so did not press him to the point of open revolt. He *was* making progress; he did co-operate—when he felt like it. He did better at swimming than at anything else and enjoyed it, so that she used a visit to the shore as a bon-bon reward for good behaviour. Their relationship became dryly tolerant on each side, with Lauren grumbling goodnaturedly at him, 'If you were a stage actor, no one could say of you that you were a quick study,' to be met by his retort of, 'And if you were half as good a teacher of physical jerks as you should be, I'd be running down to the Point and back six times before breakfast by now!' In three weeks they achieved little enough, but by that little Lauren was gratified.

So was Brian Gellhorn, praising and encouraging her out of Oliver's hearing, since Oliver, assured that he was better, was apt to retort sullenly, 'Better than *what*?' refusing for his own twisted reasons to admit to any progress at all.

Dale's guarded appreciation fared even less well at Oliver's hands. 'He can think again, if he imagines he can boot me back to England before I'm ready to go,' was his repeated sour comment to Lauren whenever Dale had made the 'encouraging noises' which he claimed to despise.

Mia Sumner, grudging any attitude which might encourage the enemy, confined herself to a probing curiosity about Lauren's interest in Oliver's case. There were no impertinent questions which she hesitated to ask. Such as—

'With all the money people say your husband left you, why do you bother to work?' she queried.

'People say? Who says?' Lauren countered.

Mia shrugged. 'It gets around. Probably Dale told me. But anyway, why do you work—especially with an ungrateful curmudgeon like Oliver?'

Lauren decided to play it lightly, lest she was tempted to be rude. 'Perhaps because, like the proverbial mountain, Oliver was there,' she said.

'That's no answer. But you are saying you didn't mean to work again until Dale asked you?'

'Brian Gellhorn asked me,' Lauren corrected.

'Same thing. Brian couldn't have given you the case if Dale hadn't agreed.'

'Oliver is of age. He could have sought some further help for himself, if he'd wanted to,' Lauren pointed out.

'While battening on Dale, under Dale's roof? What a hope he'd stir a finger while he could play old man of the sea on Dale's back! No, Dale had to get things moving, that's obvious. And naturally——' Mia's tone took on a calculating drawl—— 'that pleased you if—just *if*—you had any—er—extra ambitions beyond being given Oliver's case?'

Lauren denied, 'The case wasn't even one ambition of mine. I was going back to England when it was offered, but I took it for its interest's sake.'

'With Dale as bonus prize? Or did Dale come first, and the "interest" of Oliver's case later? Because really, you know, it's all rather obvious—your not needing a job, not looking for one, but Dale being who he is, what he is, and as far as most people know, unattached—well, it must have looked like too good a chance to miss. Living here in his house, on the spot day *and* night, and probably able to spin out the case indefinitely—why, what merry widow, even one with money of her own, would have passed it up?'

The smile with which Mia might have hoped to disarm the pure mischief of the taunt chilled Lauren's very blood.

'I'd like to think you're joking, but I'm afraid you're not,' she said. 'Tell me, are you working on some fantastic theory of your own as to why I'm here, or is it another example of "People say"?'

'You can't stop them talking!'

'Who? And where?'

'All over. At the Hollands' drinks party yesterday——'

'I don't even *know* the Hollands!'

'Yes, well, it didn't amount to much. Just one of the men wondering aloud why a "lovely young heiress" like you should bother with Oliver Ransome, unless——'

'Yes? Unless——?' Lauren pressed.

'Oh, all that I've just told you is being said. I don't have to repeat it, do I?'

'No. You've made it quite clear that I'm being talked about by your friends. But you heard them—couldn't you have told them they were wrong?'

'I? How could I?' Mia's eyes widened innocently. 'After all, to tell you the truth I've had the same idea myself. For all I know you might have thought there would be something in it for you.'

'Even might think so still?' Lauren prompted.

'What do you mean?'

'Well, you've been here just as long as I have, and in that time have I shown any signs of regarding Mr Ransome as anyone other than my patient's brother?'

'Not that I remember. But would you—in front of me?'

'Or,' Lauren pursued, 'known him to treat me as anyone other than Oliver's physiotherapist?'

'Same answer as before—would he be likely to, in front of me?' Mia paused. 'If he were interested, that is——'

'Which you can take it from me, he isn't.'

'And you should know, one supposes. Though on your side at least, I'd have said it shows.'

'What shows?'

Mia's hand made a vague gesture. 'Something. When a woman is interested in a man, it shows. Mean to say you don't find Dale—exciting? That he has no—what's the "in" word for it?—charisma for you? And here's a question you ought to answer—— If you aren't, and never have been, attracted by him, why should you go so upstage at the suggestion you might want him?'

Lauren did not reply for a moment. But when her retort occurred to her, she was rather pleased with it.

'Perhaps,' she said silkily, 'it's because I understand there are and have been so many competitors for Dale Ransome's favours that I'd rather not have it supposed I'm standing in line on the odd chance of his throwing a few my way!'

Which might have reassured Mia that in Lauren she hadn't a rival for Dale, but which, Lauren hoped, had left her discomfited too.

CHAPTER SEVEN

FOR the last week of her stay on the island Mia went to some American friends on a neighbouring estate. Her brittle, restless presence was no loss to the house. Even Hector and Melie seemed to relax, Melie in particular sighing, 'Missus Sumner always *want*. Want this, want that; Melie, will you fetch; Melie, would you bring. No, Melie, not that one— the other—— Know exercise good for a person, Missus Sumner; keep 'm on the go!' Dale dined more often at home and Oliver made a more willing third at the table if Mia were not there.

He was making some progress. With some labour he could lever himself from his chair, and when he cared to try, he could move with two sticks, dragging his leg round in a half-circle to take a step forward.

'When you can bend that knee,' Lauren encouraged him, 'you'll be *walking*. I suppose you couldn't make yourself a deadline for achieving that?'

'No, I could not,' he retorted, his voice thick with effort. 'Deadlines are your business, not mine. It was your idea you could put me on my feet in a matter of weeks——'

'And you are!'

'Huh! A baby of a year old can *stand*.'

'And given the will to walk, will do it before too

119

long. What you're lacking is the will, young man. Come on now—move!'

'Why?'

'For once, because I say so,' she replied patiently. She retreated a few paces back from him. 'Now—get *to* me.'

Though her massage and support of him at exercises were physically tiring, she was always more strained by the mental effort of combating his sullen despairs and bolstering his will. She had known it would be like this; she had been through it before with patients who had lost their faith and their hope, and couldn't raise any charity towards the people round them either. Sympathy Oliver distrusted, and open censure enraged him. She found an abrasive, confident chivvying of him the best way to deal with him. He reacted to it angrily, with set teeth, but if he were sufficiently needled by its challenge, he did respond.

At the end of a session with him Lauren almost always needed to relax, and was glad to be able to, alone in the garden or on the shore. As Oliver mastered his one-sided swimming motion and was encouraged and healthily wearied enough to allow Hector to take him back to the cottage without her, she sometimes stayed behind to sunbathe and swim again.

There was no glittering Mia to disturb her, no cryptic, withdrawn Dale. The cove was private to Mont Michel, and no one came to it uninvited. She would almost be safe to bathe in the nude, but not quite daring this, she compromised by lying on the sand with her one-piece suit drawn down to her waist, toasting back and front in turn.

People had been right: the sandflies did not trouble her now. She could think or doze in perfect peace with only the tiny lap-lap of the surf for lullaby ...

This afternoon she lay prone, her head resting sideways on her bent arms for pillow, her wide-brimmed straw hat covering the burn-vulnerable nape of her neck. She closed her eyes and drifted off luxuriously. When she woke she would probably be too warm, but what matter? She could always go into the water again.

A sound she was too sleepy to identify disturbed her before she was ready to wake. She snuggled her face again into her arms, felt the hat slide off her shoulders, sat up with a tetchy 'Tch!' to retrieve it—and saw first the shadow on the sand, then the seated figure which cast it—Dale in swimming trunks, clasping his knees, his head turned towards her, watching her, seeing the frenzied movement of her hands in search of the drooped straps of her suit ... taking measurement of her embarrassment, and not looking away.

A hat to shade her neck, but nothing for her breasts, naked to the sun and to his gaze. Even her towel was yards away. The heat of shame swept her whole body as she managed to drag up one strap, fumbled the other.

'Please——!' she begged. 'I couldn't have known——' She was speaking to him now, lying on his back, staring up into the glare overhead.

'Believe it or not,' he said to the sky, 'I know the shape of a woman's body by now. Even'—lifting his head to glance across at her—'of yours. In the past, I admit you had me foxed at getting through your guard of maidenly modesty. But you're an older and worldlier girl now; the topless age has come in since, and a few extra inches of two-way stretch nylon can hardly be intended to *conceal*.'

'Don't!' She was remembering other shores, other times when she had changed in his presence, first warning him to 'look the other way' until she had been ready for him to come to her to slip his arms round her waist and for both of them to pretend their bodies weren't stirred in their yet-so-far nearness of decorous swimwear or tantalising beach-wrap.

'Don't what?' Dale enquired with lazy indifference. When she did not answer he lay back again, sifting sand through his outspread fingers. 'From your reaction to being surprised in a perfectly legitimate relaxation, anyone would think I'd been lurking in the bushes to seduce you, or at least to demand that you swim in the nude with me!' He paused. '*Would* you swim in the nude with me?' he added, still talking to the sky.

Lauren was covered now, kneeling up and reaching for her towel. 'No,' she said shortly.

'Cancel the lewd suggestion. Would you swim with me—period?'

'We've swum together when you've come down to help Oliver,' she reminded him.

'When you could be safe in the illusion that virtue was served by a mere rag of conventional wear which in fact does nothing at all to hide a woman's more seductive lines?'

Knowing she sounded pompous, 'It isn't a question of virtue, but of decency,' she said.

He sat up and bowed to her from the waist. 'Bravely said, Mrs Grundy!' he mocked. 'Very well, change the suggestion again—will you swim with me—now?'

'I didn't mean to go in again,' she lied.

'And when you were learning to swim, did no prankster ever pick you up bodily and throw you in when you hadn't meant to go?'

He was standing now and so was she. 'Possibly. Though if anyone tried it, I don't remember that they got away with it,' she said shortly.

'Warning me that I couldn't get away with it either?'

She avoided the glitter of challenge she had glimpsed in his eyes. 'Not referring to you. Or assuming that if you wanted to try it, you must know plenty of girls who would see it as a joke,' she said.

He sighed elaborately. 'And how right you are, at that! Only the oddball or two who'd react with the dead weight of a sack of coals, but dozens of girls, thanks be, who'd be gratifyingly thrilled!'

Mia Sumner, for one? Lauren almost questioned sourly, but bit it back when she saw him sit again and pat the sand at his side.

'And so—no mixed bathing today. Conversation must fill the gap, so let's have some, shall we?' he invited. 'Sit down.'

She hesitated, one arm in the sleeve of her beach

jacket.

'I want to talk about Oliver,' he said, all raillery gone from his tone. 'Sit *down*.'

She sat down, kneeling first, then settling sideways on one hip. This was better. This was easier. The subject of Oliver was her province and Dale could hardly sidetrack her from it into the dangerous, emotion-fraught byways which he seemed to enjoy exploring at her expense. Her quickened pulse slowed down. 'About Oliver? What?' she asked.

'Well, how is he shaping now? How long is it all going to take?'

She shook her head. 'I can't tell. It's always depended to a certain extent on how long *he* wants it to take. I made that clear, I thought.'

'Of course. But you've taken him so far physically, and doesn't the rest follow, or at least go along with that?'

'From the present stage he's reached, he'll better that, I think. But if by "the rest" you mean his mental attitude, I don't know when that might change—if it's going to at all.'

'Hm.' Dale drew sand into a mound beside him, smoothing and patting it flat. 'If Oliver were, say, a sickly lion, one might try what the stimulus of a nubile young lioness might do for him. So what about a girl or two in the offing—had you thought of that? Not too difficult to find some for him.'

'Not a hope. I hinted once that he had only to lift a finger and they'd come flocking. But if one dared to try, he'd think she'd been put up to it or was pitying him, and I wouldn't answer for the result. While his lameness makes him feel inferior he's "agin" our sex, as he's "agin" a lot of other things. He tolerates me because I'm less a female than I am a robot taskmaster. But look how rude he can be to Miss Sumner!'

'There's no need to quote Mia in this connection. They're not in the same league at all,' Dale snapped to that.

(Because she's your girl, and even poor Oliver mustn't aspire to her or dislike her?) Thinking it but saying nothing, Lauren watched Dale add more height and bulk to his sandpile, level off its top and scrabble out a ditch to surround it before he asked, 'What gives you the idea Oliver doesn't see you as a woman?'

'I'm pretty sure he doesn't. Nor must he,' she added quickly.

'Why not? I thought the essence of successful psychiatry was in the patient's falling for his or her practitioner?'

'You've been listening to old wives' tales. Anyway, I'm a physiotherapist, not a psychiatrist,' she retorted.

'But you use psychiatry. You've boasted of doing so.'

'Maybe. When it's necessary.'

'As you assumed—rightly, it seems—it would be with Oliver.' Dale paused. Then: 'When you've done all you think you can for his physical case—by which time he may be walking?—do you plan then to go back to England?'

Surprised by the apparently off-beam question, Lauren puzzled, 'I think so. Why do you ask? That is, I'm afraid I'd consider I'd failed if I went, having cured him *only* physically.'

'Having made the mistake of discouraging him from thinking of you as an attractive woman?'

Lauren stared. 'The *mistake*?' she echoed.

More sand was patted on to the castle. The ditch was deepened. 'Might it not be one?' Dale asked. 'You're the only person with whom Oliver has any kind of civil relationship, so if you let it become something closer, mightn't that bear results?'

Had she heard aright? 'Let's get this straight,' she said slowly. 'You're suggesting I encourage Oliver to fall in love with me in order to lift his spirits?'

'He need only *think* himself in love with you. I imagine the sickly lion would only need a temporary spur to his sexuality, so that once Oliver responded, you might not be embarrassed by his calf-love for long. But if he knows he's going to lose you to England, he could be readier to make England his objective too. You see my line of reasoning?'

Lauren nodded. 'I do indeed. May I recap? You naturally want to get Oliver to England for further treatment. Equally naturally, you'd be glad to be rid of me, and if both objects could be gained by my vamping him—always supposing I could—you're only concerned about *my* embarrassment. You couldn't care less what it would do to him?'

'It would be an experience, and he'd get over it.'

'If it happened, it could make him very unhappy while it lasted. And if you don't know that, you must have forgotten what being in love is like,' she returned tartly.

'And as I've remarked before, I very much

doubt whether you've *ever* known what it's like.
All right, forget it. It was just an idea which I
thought might hurry matters up in getting him over to
England, which is of the first importance to me.'

Lauren agreed, 'Of course. He's a self-invited
encumbrance, and you've the right to your own
house for yourself and your guests——'

'—Which he knows very well, and makes the
denial of it to me one of his chief weapons.' Dale
stood and brushed sand from his thighs and legs
and offered a hand absently to help her up. 'Perhaps it's as well he doesn't realise I have an even
more urgent reason for seeing the back of him as
soon as may be.'

Lauren looked up as she scrambled to her feet.
'You have? Ought I to know it?'

'You ought not,' he said shortly. 'You wouldn't
approve.'

'I'm sorry, I only thought——'

'That you could use it in persuasion of him? No.
You must manage on the facts you have. I'm not
entrusting it to you at this stage, and if that huffs
you, Brian doesn't know it either.'

Lauren accepted this in silence as she watched
him kick his sand castle apart. 'What was that
meant to be?' she asked.

'A symbol—an impregnable citadel surrounded
by an unfordable moat. No drawbridge provided,
you'll observe.'

She met her cue. 'And so—a symbol of what?'

'Could be the kind of woman who makes duty
and rectitude and iron-strict loyalties into a bul-
wark against the temptations and desires to which

ordinary folk succumb, wouldn't you say?'

'Meaning me?' She had to look away to hide the hurt in her eyes.

'If the cap fits. And if ever there were a draw-bridge across *your* moat, seems you took it up long ago and threw away the keys—right?'

'That's not fair!' she protested. 'Aren't you ever going to forget the past?'

Dale shrugged. 'Probably—in my grave. But scars only fade, they never completely disappear, however long cured the wound. Even if only in a medical context, you should know that,' he accused.

'Of course I know that. But doesn't it occur to you that at the time of our—our parting, my wound and my scars could cut just as deep as yours? And the scars have lasted just as long?'

Would he understand she was pleading her case? Asking his future mercy, if not the impossibility now of his love? It was to seem he did not, or wilfully would not when he looked her over with pseudo-admiration.

'Have they really? If so, they must be in some place which doesn't show. Aren't you lucky?' he mocked.

That bizarre suggestion of Dale's, that she might speed up Oliver's recovery by persuading him she was desirable! The more she wondered about it, the more Lauren's distaste for it increased. Dale had discussed it as detachedly as if he were merely recommending a different clinical treatment. But could he ever have thought it viable? Surely not? He must then have been using it as a signal to her that, though he admitted to 'scars', he had written

off even the nuisance value of their having met
again; that he was now giving his blessing to a new
affair for her, even one with his brother, as a roué
who had tired of a mistress might willingly pass
her on to one of his friends!

The thought was enraging, but was more likely, she
felt, than that he could have believed she would
connive at offering herself to Oliver as an incentive to
his agreement to return to England. Though as if,
anyway, Oliver could be seduced or cajoled into
falling in love to order! Someone, thought Lauren
scornfully, should remind Dale Ransome that you
could take horses to the water—and the rest.

Mia Sumner was not to return to Mont Michel
before she left St Just, but Lauren's hopes that
they needn't meet again were dashed when Brian
and Marthe urged her to accept the invitation of
Mia's hostess to a charity fancy dress party on the
last night of Mia's stay.

'You must come,' said Marthe Gellhorn on the
telephone. 'Mrs Page-Broome is a splendid organi-
ser of parties and she does much for the island
charities. This one is to send some convalescent
children to Disneyland at Orlando in Florida, as you
will have seen from the card you will have had.
Everyone, but everyone, as they say, will be there!'

'You're going yourselves?'

'But naturally!' Marthe chirruped.

'And "Remembrance of Things Past"?' asked
Lauren, reading from her invitation-card. 'What
does that mean?'

'Oh, that's a title Hannah Page-Broome has
lifted from Proust,' Marthe explained. 'It is the

theme of the party, do you see? We are all to dress as people from the Caribbean's past. Famous characters or ordinary people, it does not matter, as long as we do not go as ourselves. You will be there?'

'If I can think of a costume,' Lauren promised.

'You must have dinner with us on the night, and change here. We'll come for you,' Marthe promised.

Surprisingly it was Melie who suggested a costume for Lauren. 'You all-dark like us, missus. You make like Caribbean gal of old time—not like now, all 'Murrican shirts and pants like men,' Melie pronounced. 'You tie gay ribbon bows in hair and wear petticoats—many and bright. Bright like flowers— red and yellow and all colours. And wide—wide, so that you can flick-flick like this, when the boys are looking——' she demonstrated with a sexy twirl of her own working skirt which made Lauren laugh.

The idea appealed to her as she felt she should leave Caribbean history to the people who knew more about it than she did. 'But where could I get the dress?' she asked.

'I take you shop in town. Gals dress up this way carnival time, and madam of shop, she make up ribbon and feather headpiece for you—all perky. Do as I show you too, and no one guess at party you not *real* Caribbean native gal,' urged Melie.

The shopping expedition was a success. Melie approved several layers of garish scarlet and gold and blue skirting, mounted for contrast on a black lace bodice barred with velvet. The wisp of bonnet-cum-topknot which was fashioned for Lauren while they waited was based on a square of material, stuck with a few feathers and knotted into a tiny cap to pin to her hair.

How to arrange her hair was a problem until, preparing for the dress rehearsal on which Melie insisted, she had an idea . . . an idea and a memory.

In the days when Dale had loved her and for long afterwards from habit, she had worn a rather childish centre parting and a fringe. If she could manage that again——? She found that she could; the topknot sat jauntily to the side of the crown of her head and there was an echo of Dale's teasing about her dark gipsy looks in her ears.

In fact Marthe fetched her for both luncheon and dinner on the day. In the afternoon they lazed in the garden and Marthe offered thumbnail sketches of Mrs Page-Broome's probable guest list and the costumes they were likely to choose.

'The Empress Josephines will be lucky if there are not at least three of them,' she chuckled. 'She was born in Guadaloupe, you know. And Lord Nelson is sure to be there—in duplicate too, perhaps. And Toussaint L'Ouverture, who founded Haiti. Someone will go as Sam Lord, the wrecker, and someone else will be an *obeah* man, pretending to practise voodoo. Brian will be a past French Governor of St Just, and I the Governor's Lady, in an Empire gown and false ringlets. What are you wearing yourself?'

Lauren told her.

'And Dale? He is coming too?'

Lauren said she thought so, though dressed as whom she did not know. As soon as they arrived themselves—late because Brian had been kept at the hospital—she looked out for him, and saw him with their hostess and Mia.

Mia was slimly statuesque in a low-cut Grecian robe and a Grecian coiffure. 'I think she is Pauline, Napoleon's sister who employed slaves to build herself a palace on Haiti. Some artist, I forget who, painted or sculpted her like that,' said Marthe. 'But Dale—who is he?'

For Lauren he was simply Dale—tautly virile and scarcely in disguise except for the ragged stocking cap on his brown hair. For the rest he wore knee-high boots, a swagger of black breeches, a woollen shirt open to the waist, where a broad swathe of red cloth was knotted sashwise, the ends hanging down his thigh. He was as earthy and carnal as Mia was aloofly classic, and Lauren was glad. Whatever character he was meant to be, at least he was as ordinary and as of-the-people as she was herself.

'Let's go over and join them,' Marthe offered. 'In any case, we ought to pay our respects to Mrs Page-Broome.'

They did so. Mrs Page-Broome, herself a buxom Empress Josephine, moved off to greet other guests, and Marthe offered her cheek for Dale's kiss. She told Mia she might just have stepped off the artist's canvas, and asked Dale, 'We have been wondering who you are—tell?'

'Just an item in a crowd scene; one of the other ranks,' he said. 'A member of the *boucaniers* outlawed in the mountains when the Spaniards were ravaging the island.'

'Oh—yes.' Marthe explained to Lauren, 'They were rebels who poached cattle and sheep and camped in the hills and harassed the Spanish however they could. They spit-roasted their meat over a *boucan*, Creole for an open fire, and so—*boucaniers*. In English—what?' she appealed to Dale.

'Buccaneers,' he supplied. 'And you?'

'Consort to the Governor some time when we were in French hands. I have borne him seven children and buried three. Do I look the part?' she laughed, smoothing hips and stomach padded amply with scatter cushions and steadying her top-heavy headdress of artificial fruit and flowers.

Mia was looking at Lauren with as much interest in another woman's appearance as she ever allowed herself. 'A true child of the people. Very authentic,' she murmured. Smiling as at a private joke, she added, 'But whoever put you up to it was a *little* too cruel. Don't you agree, Dale? Marthe?'

Marthe stared. 'What do you mean?'

'My dear!' Mia's slight nod was at Lauren's absurd little cap. 'Her *madras*—the tying of it in a one-point! Too bad of you, Marthe, not to warn her what it means. And Dale, *you* must know too!'

'What——?' In puzzled dismay Lauren put her hand to her cap, tracing the one corner of the material which had been tweaked and knotted to stand upright in a saucy peak. 'This, you mean?' she asked them all. 'Have I committed a fearful gaffe? What *is* the joke?'

Marthe said, 'Pff! That's all it is—a joke. Your *madras* is charming.'

Mia added, her glance measuring Lauren's gaudy dress, 'And quite in keeping, if you mean to act accordingly. But all the same——! Dale, oughtn't I to tell her that a one-point tied *madras* is read as an open invitation to the men, telling them that a girl is—available?'

Lauren felt, rather than saw, Dale's scrutiny of the hot colour flooding her face. He said drily, 'Whether or not you ought, you seem to have told her,' and Marthe scoffed,

'Nonsense! It has always only meant that a Creole girl isn't engaged.' To which Mia agreed smoothly,

'That too, of course. But everyone knows— don't they?—that the camp-followers to the armies always wore the one-point as a kind of badge of their profession. And surely, I thought, Lauren would hardly care to——?' She left the rest of the suggestion in the air.

Lauren began, 'I wasn't to know——' only for Marthe to blaze in her defence.

'*Chérie*, there was nothing *to* know, except by "*Honi soit . . .*" kind of thinkers. You are in costume—have fun in it! Here——!' she signalled to Brian, approaching in gold and scarlet braided coat and black silk knee-breeches, 'come and ask Lauren for the first dance, and see that she doesn't lay a finger on her *madras* at your peril! Me, I am taking Dale!' And with a provocative little *chassée* she went into Dale's arms, and whirled him away, without a backward glance at Mia, left standing alone.

Brian asked Lauren, 'What was that about your *madras*?'

'Nothing. Just something silly.'

'But what?'

She told him, and he laughed. 'Think nothing of it. But trust Mia Sumner to enjoy making another woman lose face! I'm inclined to agree with Oliver that she's a poisonous type, and I don't understand why Dale, who's pretty astute on character, doesn't see through her.'

'Perhaps they're too close for him to get her into focus,' Lauren suggested waspishly.

Brian laughed again. 'That could be said of Dale's relations with other and earlier women than Mia. He *grapples* them to him, but he hasn't married one of them yet.'

'Is he going to marry Mia eventually, though?'

'Heaven forbid! He'll plummet in my estimation of his sense if he does. But no, I should doubt if he'd think of it, at least while he still has Oliver on his back. The feud between those two is nothing short of cat-and-dog, and Dale must realise the hell he would create for himself by importing Mia permanently to Mont Michel.' Brian paused. 'By the way, and talking shop to you, which I shouldn't at a party—what report on Oliver am I to send back to his father via Dale this time?'

'This time?' Lauren echoed absently, her mind busy on the conviction that Brian had unwittingly supplied her with the clue to Dale's 'other' and secret urgency to be rid of Oliver. For his own sake, he wouldn't marry Mia until Oliver had gone. He thought Brian didn't know it, but Brian had guessed it might be so, and now she knew too——! She jerked back to the present to hear Brian re-echoing, 'This time, yes. When Dale goes to England next week—or didn't you know he was going?'

'He hasn't told me yet. Is he flying or going by sea?'

'Flying, for speed, I should think. Of course you

and I must put our heads together on a formal clinical report for the Old Man, but off the cuff, what hopes can we give Dale now? Let's drop out and talk about it over a drink at the bar, may we?'

When they parted Lauren felt she had made a good case for their continuing with Oliver on the lines she had established.

'Give me time; make Dale give me time,' she had begged Brian. 'Physically I know he'll improve, and though I can't promise any breakthrough in his mood, it could come in time, or even suddenly, if there were anything—though I don't know what—to trigger it off.'

Brian had agreed, and later in the evening she was to tell herself she mustn't hope too much of a meeting by coincidence with an English girl she didn't know.

They were alone together in the cloakroom. The girl, in a panniered dress and a mob-cap ('I am a lady-in-waiting to the Empress'), was busy with needle and thread, re-sewing a buckle on her shoe. 'You're at Mont Michel, treating Oliver Ransome, aren't you?' she asked Lauren. 'Mrs—Napier, is that right? Yes? Well, I'm Cherry Huppert. My parents are dead, and I live with one aunt in England and spend a month out here every year with my other aunt, Mrs Valery. Do you know her?'

'I've met her, I think,' said Lauren.

'Yes, well, at home we're neighbours of the Ransomes at Charter Court, and I've known Oliver—Dale too, of course—since I was so high. Except when we were at boarding school, Oliver and I were always together. I left school last year and came out here as usual, but I'd gone back before Oliver's car had that crash, with Dale driving.' She looked up from her stitching. 'Mean to say Oliver's never mentioned me?'

'He's told me very little about himself or his friends in England,' Lauren said guardedly.

The young face clouded. 'But I was special! *We* were special. He can't have forgotten me in less than a year. Look, will you tell him I'm here, and that you've asked me to see him?'

'I'd rather he asked you himself,' said Lauren.

'But will he? I've written to him, but he doesn't answer. So how would it be if I just turned up one day and said "Booh!"'

Lauren laughed. 'You could, I suppose. But just as he doesn't answer letters, he isn't always civil.'

'I wouldn't expect him to be. We've always fought like tiger cats, but it doesn't mean a thing.' The sewing thread was bitten off and the shoe was put on. 'All right,' said the girl, 'don't breathe my name to him, and I'll arrive. And if I can't shake some sense into him, no one can. For one thing, he owes it to Old Man Ransome to come home, and I'll stand no nonsense from him about refusing, as they say he does. Anyway, thank you, I'm glad we met. See you!' And eighteenth-century panniers, mob-cap, buckled shoes and twentieth-century confident brashness whisked away with a loud bang of the cloakroom door.

Lauren drew a long breath. So! *Would* the abrasive scorn of a teenager like himself succeed with Oliver where she and Dale and Brian had so far failed? She feared not. Why should it? But there *had* been a diehard determination about Cherry Huppert which just might turn the key of Oliver's obstinate will.

And if it did—Lauren looked further—what would it mean to herself and to Dale?

For him—freedom from the prison which his conscience-stricken care for Oliver had built around him. Freedom to marry Mia if he meant to. Even freedom from the irk of such dependence as he had upon Lauren's own skills with Oliver. Freedom——

And for her? Freedom too of a sort. Freedom to write *Closed* across the half success, half failure of Oliver's case. Freedom to leave St Just, her original silly deception still unguessed by anyone but Brian. Freedom to buy that economy air ticket back to England. Freedom to leave Dale again in her past, where he once was, and where—some day—she might learn to forget him.

And in her sore heart she wanted no part in any of it—*none*.

CHAPTER EIGHT

THE party took its course of chatter and movement
and laughter through to midnight and beyond,
when, as it was a charity occasion which would
make news, it culminated in a series of historical
tableaux, arranged primarily for the local journal's
photographers, but where the amateur cameras
flashed and clicked for a long time as well.

At last it broke up. Mrs Page-Broome was congratulated warmly on its success; crinolines and
flounces and plumed hats and sword-scabbards
were tucked into cars which swept away in convoy,
seen off by Mrs Page-Broome and her house
guests, Mia, exquisite and ethereal, among them.

Lauren had expected Brian to drive her back to
Mont Michel, but as she and Marthe had waited
for him to bring up his car, Dale drove up in his.

'I'll take Lauren,' he had told Marthe. 'Then
you and Brian can go straight home.'

'Never felt less like going "straight home".
Lovely party,' Marthe had laughed. But Dale had
already opened his car door for Lauren, and she
had got in.

While they waited in the queue of departing
cars, it occurred to her that she ought to tell him
she had invited Cherry Huppert to freely visit his
house, and when they were clear of the queue and
on their way, she told him.

He appeared to approve; asked, 'Are you going to tell Oliver she's coming?'

'He must know she's here. She's written to him without any reply. But no, she doesn't want him told. She plans to surprise him. She sounded a pretty forthright young woman; she could be good for him,' Lauren added.

'Or could get thrown out on her ear for keeps.'

'I've warned her of that. What was their relationship in England?' Lauren asked curiously. 'Was there any romance to it?'

'Only if their "not speaking" for a lot of the time spells romance. What terms they were on in between their hassles, I don't know.'

'What interests had they in common?'

'Horses. And riding.'

'Riding? Oh dear!'

'Meaning it's not going to be on for him?'

'It could be—much later. But not yet.'

'Then his interest in horseflesh will have to be at secondhand until it is,' said Dale. 'He and the Huppert girl had made the National Stud Book their bedside reading since they were fourteen, and there wasn't a racehorse currently running of which they couldn't recite the form. That's an exaggeration, of course, but there was show-jumping and cross-country horse trials for them too.'

'Yet Oliver has never mentioned any of it to me,' Lauren puzzled. 'Have you ever tried to talk to him about it?'

'With no success. I might have been speaking Chinese. But the Huppert girl should be allowed a try.' Dale took a sharp hairpin bend on the narrow road before he spoke again. Then, entirely out of context, he asked, 'Quoting Marthe, have *you* "never felt less like going straight home"?'

'I?' Her instinct had recognised invitation in the question, but how was she to answer it?

She said, 'Well, you are driving me home with you, aren't you? Have I any choice?'

'I'm offering you one. Or, if you would prefer to keep up the fiction, a common *boucanier* is inviting an attractive camp-follower to see his mountain retreat. Highly desirable residence, built of natural materials, no modern conveniences, but privacy from the enemy guaranteed. What do you say?'

'You mean,' she hesitated, 'there is—are still—places in the hills where the rebels used to hide out? They've been preserved as they were then? And you can take a car to them?'

Dale shook his head. '"Preserved" is hardly the word. They're not on the tourist sights lists. I only learned of this one from an old man whose great-grandfather was himself a *boucanier*. And we can't take the car all the way. We have to leave it below and do the last paths on foot. What kind of shoes are you wearing?'

'A sort of sabot thing, very stout.' Caution was clamouring, *Pretend you can't walk in them. Say you're too tired. Tell him anything* . . . anything but the truth that if he hadn't meant his suggestion or took it back now, she would not be far from tears of childish disappointment.

She couldn't afford to listen to caution. For once Dale was not mocking her nor blaming her, but offering her a hand to a small adventure, as he used to in the old days. In imagination she was back there with him—taking his dare to a high dive, racing him and always losing, pretending to rebel against him and being kissed into submission to his will—she had been able to trust him then, and for the sake of her aching desire to be alone with him for a little longer, she was going to trust him now.

Besides, a dark imp of jealousy was also working against caution. Mia had monopolised him for most of the evening, and Mia deserved to be punished for that cruel gratuitous insult at her expense. Mia would have him again at their chosen time and place. But tonight for a very little while there would be Lauren and Dale, and if she were lucky, Dale allowing her to pretend the in-between past had never happened.

Taking her agreement for granted, he turned the car on to the nearest mountain road, where it lurched and bumped on the deeply rutted surface, climbing all the time. The great trees and ferns of the rain forest made a canyon of the road until it became a mere track and then no way ahead at all. Dale stopped, took a torch from the glove box and helped Lauren out.

'Give me your hand.' She put hers into his, not daring to question his unexpected willingness to spend unnecessary time with her on this bizarre enterprise. In order to make the most of it she decided recklessly to go along with the makebelieve he had suggested. They weren't Dale Ransome and Lauren Napier who had once been sweethearts; they were two nameless peasants of another age for whom these rough ways and this darkness would have been commonplace.

He brushed aside thorn branches and clinging lianas, going slightly ahead of her, though still hand in hand. As if he had read her thoughts, he said, 'If you'd agreed to visit us in camp, girl-of-the-town, you couldn't have expected us to do more than leave you a lantern down below and let you find your own way up.'

Her blood chilled at thinking which had gone further than her own, but it was too late to step out of character now, and she forced a laugh. 'Chivalry not being included in the invitation?' she asked.

'Chivalry taking second place to necessity, for men finding themselves without women for months on end; the cynical reasoning being, I daresay, that if you didn't find your way to camp, another girl would,' he retorted. 'But if you persevered and came the whole way, probably you were paid well for your services—— Come, we're nearly there.' He shone the torch on a rock face, stark against a dark backcloth of trees. 'Inside that,' he said.

'*In* it?'

'A cave, well curtained in front, and sheer cliff behind. Impregnable from there and no surprise possible from the front.' Going forward, Dale lifted a thick fall of foliage, and when she joined him, let it fall behind them.

At first the darkness was complete. Then the torch ranged red walls, roof and floor, the latter carpeted with dry fronds powdering to dust.

Lauren suppressed a shiver. 'It's cold,' she said. 'Where would you have had your camp-fire—your *boucan*?'

'Outside. It would have smoke-dried us in here. But we fed well when we managed to win a goat or a calf, and we bedded down cosily enough. And we did get rid of the Spaniards in the end, after all.'

'Yes—well, thank you for showing it to me. For its—I mean your purpose, it must have been perfect.' She moved about, touching the walls and scuffing the brown carpet, thinking as she did so that this was the end of the game. Now they would go back to being themselves, her snatched companionable hour with him behind her. 'We'd better go.'

But Dale had lifted his head and was listening. 'In *that*?' he questioned of the thunderous drumbeat of Caribbean rain which could erupt without even the warning of seconds, flood areas to lakes within minutes, and cease as suddenly as if a heavenly tap had been turned off.

Lauren listened too. 'But we can't stay here. It could last for hours!'

'Sorry. We're staying.' Dale stooped to scoop the rough litter of fronds into some semblance of a hassock. 'Sit down. As you say, it could be a long wait.'

Having no choice, obediently she sat, and he lounged beside her, resting on an elbow. Just so, after clearing away a picnic meal, they would have settled down on the loose straw fallen from a haystack or in the shade of a spreading tree, close enough to touch and to look and to confide dreams.

It seemed that Dale was remembering too, for he asked, 'Used you and Steven Napier to go hedging and ditching when he was courting you?'

'No. He was rarely well enough to walk very far. And he'd given up driving when he'd been warned he might collapse at the wheel.'

'So your outings were chauffeur-driven affairs, tables set up to take white cloths and luncheon hampers from Harrods?'

Lauren shook her head at the intentional gibe of that. 'No. We didn't go on picnics at all. The out-of-doors had never appealed to Steven very much.'

'Cheating you of your birthright of romantic moonlight and love among the heather? No wonder your natural springs dried up.'

'My——? What do you mean?' But she knew, and showed it by her lowered head and her restless fingering of the litter. He had accused her often enough of not knowing what it was to love, and now he had told her so again. Equally often she had retorted that he was unfair, and he hadn't heeded. But—could she perhaps *show* him? He had let her pretend to the character of a light-o'-love who would find the seduction of a man easy. So supposing she made the first advance, would he respond? And if he did, what might the aching need of her kisses be able to tell him?

Her heart thumping with sick excitement, as lightly as she could she said, 'You aren't playing our game properly. Remember I'm only a camp-follower who doesn't have to *feel* any natural urges; she only has to act them.'

Dale had switched off the torch, but now he turned it on again, full in her face. 'Aren't you on rather dangerous ground?' he asked. 'If that was an invitation, supposing I took you up on it?'

She managed a slight shrug. 'I'm here. You are. And it's raining. Could I help myself?' She allowed a moment's pause. 'Even if I wanted to?' she added.

'Or if I cared to let you try——' His voice had thickened; he was kneeling up, thigh to thigh with her; she knew what was coming and steeled herself for it. He was warning her that she had tempted him too far, and that he was prepared to be rough with her. But she promised herself to surprise him with her lack of resistance. Let him once take her in his arms, even if she shocked him with abandon, she had somehow to get through to him that all she had promised him in love in the past was his for the taking still. She *had* to let him know!

Still kneeling, he took her face between his hands, his eyes levelling with hers in the darkness to which they were becoming used.

'Very well, little professional,' he met her challenge, 'since we've nothing more pressing to do until the rain stops, let's sample your wares, may we? Come——'

Though a shudder went through her as his arms went about her, she arched her body to draw closer to him, and parted her lips in greedy welcome to his kiss when his mouth found and took hers demandingly.

He lifted his head once and looked a question at

her, but she drew him to her again with a little whimper of reluctance to let him go.

His hands wandered, explored, tried conclusions with her velvet-barred bodice which defeated him until, laughing at his efforts, she untied the confining laces and made him free of her bare shoulders and the swell and deep cleavage of her breast. He pressed her back on to the litter and aligned his body beside hers. She knew she had aroused him, and should have been ashamed of the deliberation she had brought to it. But when you loved, wantonness came easily, was delightful, and she touched and caressed and enjoyed with all the sensual desire within her. She had sloughed her role as commercial temptress now; now her abandonment, her love-play with him, her pleasure in his body, were all her own, and if he asked the ultimate of her, she would give it exultingly. For then, surely, if not already, she must have shown him how ardently she wanted him; wanted *him* alone, the one man who mattered to her world.

When she knew with all certainty that they shared the same primitive need, she would be ready with her eager, 'Yes ... *yes*!' and he would know ...

But suddenly it was over. His hands ceased their arousal of her, fell away, then pulled her roughly to sit. He stood himself, looking down at her. 'All right,' he rasped, 'that's enough. You've proved you can play the harlot to a very nice point of conviction—almost. Congratulations. Too bad, wasn't it, that I was under-rehearsed?'

Lauren cowered, realising she had failed. She

had planned it differently. Even if, she had thought, in the aftermath of their consummated lovemaking, he had momentarily questioned her passion, she could have blurted out her confession of love and deception in his arms, and he would have understood. But, undeceived, he had withdrawn too soon, and in face of the rapier of his scepticism the words of pleading stuck in her throat.

'I—I wasn't——' She stopped.

'Weren't acting superbly? You could have fooled me, if I didn't know you hadn't that amount of natural heat within you.' As she scrambled to her feet, he flicked the dangling cord of her bodice lacings. 'You'd better make yourself decent, or you might find your titillation of a sex-deprived outlaw bearing results you wouldn't like.'

She tried—once. 'Dale——?' she appealed. But he took no notice, and when she had brushed herself down she went to stand apart from him, leaning against the wall of the cave, praying that the rain would soon stop.

When it did, as suddenly as ever, he came over to her and without a word of warning, picked her up, an arm beneath her knees, the other behind her shoulders. 'After that lot, you'll be squelching and delaying us beyond my patience,' he said to her struggle of protest. 'Keep still and use the torch as intelligently as you can.'

That was all until, staggering and plunging and occasionally cursing, he reached the car and put her into her seat. By the time they arrived at the house, still in silence, Lauren had recovered enough of her poise to realise they had to achieve at least the appearance of normality.

'Brian tells me you're going to England next week. Is that so?' she asked.

'Down to Barbados first—on Sunday.'

'You'll be seeing Brian before you go—to take my report on Oliver to Mr Ransome? Will you be flying?'

'Back, yes. Out from this side, probably no. *Chaconia Lady* will be docking on Tuesday, and Mia, who's going over too, prefers to go by sea. Shall I convey your compliments to Captain Kitchin?'

'Please.'

There was nothing then but to bid him goodnight with a conventional murmur of thanks for his escort of her. He went to garage the car, leaving her to the havoc of her thoughts, in which shame and frustration and jealousy were paramount.

He was going to England with Mia, and in order to meet Mia's preferences they were sailing in *Chaconia Lady*. That they had to travel in *her* ship of high hopes and her re-meeting with Dale was the last straw to Lauren's camel load of misery that night.

Cherry Huppert's strategy was one of complete surprise. She had not warned even Lauren she was coming when she arrived one morning on Oliver's porch with as indifferent a 'Hi!' as if they had last met only yesterday.

Lauren stopped directing his exercises to exclaim with affected gaiety, 'Why, look who's here!'

Oliver demanded of Cherry, 'Who sent for you?' and then of Lauren, 'What do you mean, look who's here? Have you two met before?'

It was Cherry who answered. 'Uh-huh. At Ma Page-Broome's charity party. Why weren't you there, you lead-swinger? And when are you coming home?'

Wow! thought Lauren in awe. Even she hadn't dared such astringency as that in trying to rally Oliver. He snapped back, 'Mind your own business!'

Cherry flapped a pacifying hand. 'O.K., O.K., I only asked. But you've missed all the Spring Meetings. If you don't come soon, you'll miss the Derby.'

Oliver was silent. Then he asked grudgingly, 'What's running?'

'A big field, so far. The winner of the Chester Vase, for one, which is usually a good tip, but we don't like his trainer. Anyway, I've been betting for you all the season, and you're thirty-five pounds, ten pence up so far.' Cherry explained to Lauren, 'We don't really bet; we couldn't until we were eighteen, but we mark our fancy for the day and keep the score.'

'How could you bet for me? How did you know what I should choose?' Oliver wanted to know.

'I shut my eyes and did it with a pin.'

'Which is as good a way of picking winners as any other, I've heard,' smiled Lauren.

'Yes, well, it's not much fun, though, doing it alone. By the way,' Cherry added casually to

Oliver, 'you remember Chuck Kincaid, the one with the ears? He's going up to Cambridge in October, but he's taking an interest in racing form and wants me to give him some tips, and he's offered to drive me to Ascot in July.'

'Well, go ahead. Go with him. What's stopping you?' Oliver snarled.

'I'd rather go with you.'

His lips set. ''Fraid I'm currently not driving.'

'But you will. Won't he?' Cherry appealed to Lauren, who said,

'He means to, though probably not to Ascot in July. But look, just let us finish this session of exercise, and I'll leave you together to talk.'

'May I stay and watch what he has to do?' begged Cherry.

'Make like a performing flea for your benefit? Get lost!' Oliver muttered.

'Oh, why not? I'm going to physical training college in the autumn, and we have to do a course of physiotherapy. I could pick up some hints!'

'Using me as your guinea-pig? No fear! She's not staying,' he told Lauren. 'Get her out.'

'I agree she'd spoil your concentration. But here's an idea,' Lauren the peacemaker offered, 'why don't you ask her to meet you down at the Point for a swim this afternoon?'

'She can come if she likes. It's a free world, isn't it?'

Cherry grinned. 'I knew you'd put out the Welcome mat! All right, I'll go now, but I'll be there.'

When she had gone Oliver asked, 'Why didn't you tell her you hoped I should drive again, not

"He means to"—as if you knew I did?'

'Because if *you* didn't mean to get well enough to drive, the whole of the rest of all this is a nonsense, and I might as well pack my bags and leave,' said Lauren.

There was a pause. Then, 'Don't do that. I should miss you,' he said.

That was all. But Lauren, hearing it as the first note of appreciation of her which he had uttered, glowed. And he gave her another surprise before she left him, when he said, 'When Dale's away, he usually cancels the English papers. But ask Hector to collect them in town as he always does, will you? I may as well look them over, I suppose.'

For which breakthrough, bless you, Cherry Huppert, Lauren thought, as she was to do often in the days which followed.

The swim at the Point became a daily date which Cherry never failed. In swimming Oliver was almost independent now; sometimes Lauren did not go down with him, knowing Cherry was sure to be there. He could walk a few steps too, and there came a red-letter day of triumph when, returning with Hector from the beach, he walked to his cottage across the lawn, *pushing his empty wheelchair*.

'Oliver!' Lauren, watching his laboured progress, could have thrown her arms round him and hugged him. He belittled the effort.

'Used the chair as a crutch; couldn't have done it without,' he puffed. But she sensed he was pleased with himself. It wasn't the beginning of the end for him. It was the beginning . . .

Cherry came often to the cottage. Sometimes she would leave in dudgeon after a quarrel with Oliver; sometimes they appeared to be heads-to-gether buddies whom nothing could part. But on the day when Cherry bypassed the cottage for the main house, asking for Lauren, Lauren had barely greeted her before she blurted out, 'Yesterday Oliver told me something awful. I could hardly believe it, and it's been worrying me all night. I asked him if you knew it, and he said of course not—no one did except Dale, and no one must.'

'Then, whatever it was, why did he tell you?' asked Lauren.

'I don't know, except that we've always shared secrets, and he'd carried this one around long enough. I suppose he trusted me with it, but it's so awful a thing, so horribly *wrong*, that I've decided I must trust you with it. May I?'

Lauren said reluctantly, 'I suppose so, if you think you ought, and if it worries you too much to keep it to yourself.'

'Well, it does,' Cherry admitted. 'Besides, it ought to come out, and Oliver should never have agreed to keep it. I told him so, and he knows it, but I suppose he'll go on until Dale—— Anyway, it's about his car crash, when Dale was supposed to be driving. But Dale wasn't——'

'You're saying that *Oliver* was, after all?' Lauren breathed.

'No, neither of them. Mia Sumner was.'

There was a silence of utter shock. Then Lauren protested, 'How could she? She wasn't there, wasn't *in* the car with them!'

Cherry nodded. 'Yes, she was. She was staying with the Page-Broomes', like this time. She'd been playing golf at the Parador links and was walking back to lunch when they caught up with her and offered her a lift. She wanted to drive the car; Dale let her, and she whooped it up all round the mountain roads like crazy. But she brought it back to within about a mile of the Page-Broomes', and after that Oliver didn't know what happened. When he came round he was on the road verge, out of the car which was way off the road, wedged against a tree. Dale was with him; he'd flagged down a car to bring help. But Mia wasn't there, and Oliver learned later that Dale had sent her off to walk home to the Page-Broomes'. She hadn't a scratch on her. So all that Oliver remembered—for a while—was Dale telling him, "Listen, *I* was driving. *I* ran out of road at this bend—you didn't, and there was no one else with us. Get that and hang on to it. Because that's our story and it's got to stick." And of course it did,' Cherry concluded. 'Dale stuck to it and made Oliver promise to, and naturally Mia held *her* tongue. Dale went to court and satisfied it as to his guilt, and after that it was the version everyone has heard and has taken as gospel, with only the three of them knowing the truth.'

For Lauren, listening, one stark ugly fact stood out. Dale had deliberately—and feloniously!— shielded Mia at the price of his own reputation, and Mia had accepted the shelter. Which to Lauren spelled a closeness between them of which she had almost been convinced, though she didn't want to believe it. There could be only one reason for Dale's having taken such a risk, and Oliver—Cherry too now—must have guessed it.

Needing to spell it out, she said, 'It sounds incredible, but I suppose Dale did it because he's in love with Mia. But Oliver isn't, far from it, so why should he have agreed to keep quiet about it?'

Cherry said, 'I asked him, and I think it was because he almost wanted to agree. He's hated Mia for hiding behind Dale, and so he decided to sit tight as a threat to her which she knew as well as he did she couldn't do anything about.'

Lauren remembered their wary circling of each other and silently agreed. She had compared them to two thieves who had fallen out, and she had not been far from the truth. Mia knew Oliver had the power to ruin her, and he, hardly able to bear the sight of her, had relished and fostered her fear of him. Lauren told Cherry, 'The doctors and other people, myself included, who've tried to explain Oliver's diehard attitude thought he was taking out his revenge on Dale for his injuries. But from this, if he's told you the truth, it seems he's been seeing Mia as the enemy, not Dale at all.'

'Dale too, partly, though not as much,' said Cherry. 'Mia wasn't much of a target except when she's been here, not in Barbados, so Oliver took it out on Dale for shielding her and forbidding him to risk the truth's coming out. But he doesn't hate and despise Dale as he despises Mia. He's only wanted to needle Dale for taking on her guilt.'

'But what's changed for Oliver now—that he should have broken whatever promise Dale demanded of him, by telling the story to you, putting himself and the whole secret into your hands?' Lauren asked.

'I think,' Cherry said naïvely, 'he may have got a bit tired of hating. He'd like to like people again without strings—especially Dale. And also because he's going to tell Dale, when he comes back, that he's decided to go to England after all.'

'He has? And how much have *you* had to do with that?'

Cherry shrugged. 'Some, maybe. But I haven't persuaded him. I told him he must make up his own mind, which he has. And it's what you've all wanted for him, isn't it?'

'Knowing it's the best chance he has of a full recovery, yes,' said Lauren. 'And Dale, to whom it must mean the most, should be very, very glad.'

'Not half as glad as Mia, to see the back of Oliver,' Cherry snickered. 'For a different reason, of course, though I bet you, if Dale marries her, and with Oliver three thousand or so miles away, she'll soon manage to forget she ever had cause to fear him.' Cherry paused to frown. 'But it's still all *wrong*, isn't it? She ought to suffer, oughtn't she?'

Lauren admitted, 'Morally, yes, I suppose. But it couldn't be put right unless the case against Dale were reopened and the judgment altered, and that could only happen if Mia confessed, or Oliver changed his evidence, and I can't see Dale standing for that.'

'Oliver wasn't called to give evidence. He was too ill, and Mia skipped back to Barbados, he says. There were no eye-witnesses; Dale pleaded guilty and paid the huge fine and the compensation for the hired car, and that was all there was to it—except all the evil gossip people talked.'

'And there would probably be worse, if the case were revived and Mia dragged into it on Oliver's word against her,' mused Lauren, thinking aloud. 'But would you say he's prepared to risk even more scandal by digging it all up again?'

Cherry shook her head. 'I doubt it very much. He said the story mustn't go any further, and he only told it to me because he needed to tell someone. No, it's my guess he isn't half as bothered now about hounding Mia as he is about getting off Dale's back. So where *do* we go from here?'

'Nowhere,' Lauren decided. 'I'll see Brian Gellhorn and tell him that, though he hasn't said so to me yet, Oliver is willing to go back to England. That's all I shall say. After that, it will be between Dale and Oliver to settle, and when Oliver's case here is closed, I shall be leaving myself.'

'Yes, all right—I see. Something I've meant to ask you,' Cherry added curiously. 'Everyone says you're madly rich and needn't work, so why did you take on Oliver's treatment in the first place?'

Taken aback by the question, Lauren had no slick answer ready. 'Oh, I don't know,' she hesitated. 'Because——'

'Yes——?' Cherry prompted.

Lauren shrugged. 'Just because, that's all.'

'I see,' Cherry said again. Sagely, almost as if she did.

CHAPTER NINE

WHEN Brian heard of Oliver's decision he was not at all inclined to agree with Lauren that it was Cherry who had worked the miracle.

'It's been your long hard grind with him that's got him to the point where he could make it,' he told Lauren. 'That, and some good Ransome sense which deserted him for the time being, for probably quite damn fool reasons we'll never know. A case of matter over mind this time, I think. You've braced him physically, and he's been able to do the rest for himself. It's justified all our hopes and work, hasn't it?'

'Yes,' said Lauren, keeping the cause of Oliver's bitternesses to herself, as she had promised Cherry she would.

'And so,' pursued Brian, 'I can get on now with the machinery—recommending and appointing the consultants he ought to see for his ongoing treatment over in England. I'll need to see Dale about that. When is he coming back this time, do you know?'

Lauren did. 'Oliver and Hector had letters from him this morning. He's due back on Wednesday—flying.'

'Right. I'll be in touch.' Brian paused. 'And you, Lauren—what *about* you now?'

'You mean when you hand over Oliver's case? Well, I shall go back to England too.'

'Still for the same daft reason as before?'

'Daft or not, for just the same reason as before.'

'That you can't bear to have it known you aren't an eccentric plutocrat, practising for the whim of it, but instead are a working girl who needs to earn her living? What shame is there in that, you tell me?' Brian protested.

Lauren agreed, 'None at all—if I'd begun by being known as a working girl. But I didn't. I—I flaunted the money I hadn't got, and who's going to forgive me for that?'

'And who,' Brian countered, 'either remembers or cares *how* you "began"? All right, all right—' he lifted a hand to stop her speaking,—'Dale does, and possibly a handful of his friends he may have told——'

'Cherry Huppert says "everyone" knows it.'

'Huh—a figure of speech. And so what? You've carried the masquerade so far quite successfully, and you needn't fear anyone will hear the truth from me.'

'I know that,' she said gratefully. 'It's just that I'm tired of it as a masquerade. I want to be free of it, to be myself again and *honest*, and I can only be that by going back to England as I've known I must, even when I was mad enough to plan it. So *please*, Brian! Anyway, why should you seem to care so much that I should stay; what can it matter to you?'

'Item by item? Well, professionally I don't want to lose an excellent practitioner; neither Marthe nor I want to lose you as a friend, and I've a hunch you might find more happiness out here than in England. Marthe would like to see you marry again, and so should I.'

Lauren's smile was difficult. 'Though with a good many more men to choose from, haven't I a better chance of that in England?'

'If you're counting by numbers and not by quality—yes, I daresay,' Brian allowed.

'And they say opportunity is a fine thing!'

'That too. Not that I imagine you've ever lacked it or ever will. If I weren't married and were a younger chap—say, of Dale's age—I'd have been putting in a bid myself!'

'Oh, Brian, you're too good to me,' she laughed shakily. 'You wouldn't do any such thing.'

'Fact,' he affirmed, 'though if Dale were in the field, I wouldn't fancy my chances.' He paused. 'For his is the kind of quality I meant I'd like for you. And yours for him, no less. But now you're going to tell me, aren't you, that wishful matchmaking of that sort doesn't get me anywhere? You're determined to leave us, aren't you?'

For all her ache to confide her love to his kindness, Lauren suppressed it and managed to quip, 'You took the words right out of my mouth. The answer is Yes to both questions.'

Brian nodded and sighed. 'Exactly. I only wondered. And—hoped,' he said.

At her first session with Oliver after Cherry's revelations, he had told Lauren of his decision to go to England, but evidently had no intention of con-

fiding to her the rest of the story of his twisted
motives which he had told to Cherry. He had said
to Lauren, yawning boredly, 'Dale isn't going to
believe I've made up my mind under my own
steam, so you can take the credit for bringing me
to the point if you like. It's all one to me.'

'Well, it isn't to me,' she had retorted sharply.
'I've been telling you all along that when the time
came for you to decide things for yourself, you
would. None of us could *make* you see the sense of
finishing your treatment in England. You had to
see it yourself—in time. So let's have no more of
the "giving credit" bit, may we?'

'I thought you would like it as a testimonial,' he
had grumbled, aggrieved. 'I'd tell Dale and Doc
and they could pass it on to your next—customer,
client, victim, whatever, and it would do you a bit
of good—no?'

Lauren had to smile at the real or pretended
naïveté of that. But before she could reply he had
added, 'But I forgot—you aren't going to need any
boosts, are you? You're rich; you're rolling in the
stuff, and you only took me on for love, right?'

'You could put it like that, though for interest's
sake would be nearer the mark.'

'Prepared to face the fearful odds of both Dale
and me, even though you didn't have to?'

Lauren had had to laugh again. '*You* were a
fearful odd, all right! As prickly as a porcupine at
first, and still can be, when you're in a needling
mood. But Dale never was. He made no difficulties
at all about my treating you, and it was his idea I
should stay here at the house, so that I could con-

centrate on you.'

'And that surprised and gratified you?'

'Well, naturally. He needn't have done it.'

'Dale being Dale, and a looker like you on his very doorstep? My good Lauren Napier, how obtuse can you get? Mean to tell me he hasn't made a hopeful pass when Mia Sumner wasn't looking? Phooey!' Oliver had scorned.

She knew she had blushed, but she hadn't had to lie. Whatever 'pass' Dale had ever made to her during these months had never been 'hopeful' of anything. It had been contempt-driven, angrily punishing, assertive of his right to humiliate her, but hopeful of anything he wanted of her—never! And she could remember only with shame that their last embraces, in the *boucan* cave, had been at her invitation and his unmistakable rejection.

And so—'Phooey to you too,' she had retorted to Oliver. 'I'm a female with a job to do, and *you* can't be serious, making Dale out to be the sex-mad fanatic which he isn't!'

'You think not? Does that mean you deny that, man-woman-wise, Dale has even noticed you're around? Or, by the same token, you haven't noticed that *he* is?' Oliver had countered.

At that, in order to check this danger-fraught catechism, she had had to lie. 'Man-woman-wise, I doubt if your brother and I would register even one degree on any romantic measuring scale,' she had said with a shrug of false indifference.

To which Oliver had murmured, 'You surprise me. Dale's naughtier instincts must be slipping,' before taking up his discarded book and continuing to read.

Lauren, defeated by a cynicism she hoped he had begun to lose, had thought it wise to leave him to it.

During the subsequent days before Dale's return she enjoyed none of the sense of achievement which Brian claimed was her right. As he said, she had laid the groundwork with Oliver which Cherry had arrived in time to exploit. But though Cherry could not know it, her triumph was Lauren's private doom. Besides, Cherry, having confided the story of Dale's and Oliver's and Mia's guilty intrigue to Lauren, seemed to have sloughed off any fear of its consequences, whereas Lauren was haunted by dread of the trouble it might yet cause—for Dale.

The ugly word 'perjury' hung over her like a cloud. Dale had perjured himself in a public court in order to shield Mia, and the thought was going to besmirch every memory of him she was going to carry away with her when she left him and the island and all its bittersweet associations for good. Meanwhile she should have been glad of the news Brian had been able to send over to the Ransome home, Charter Court. Instead she could think only in terms of a self-pitying counting of days . . .

Brian told her he and Dale were in constant touch by overseas telephone, making appointments for Oliver with the appropriate English consultants, and on the day of his return Dale had asked Brian to meet his flight and to keep time free for him before he came on to Mont Michel. If his flight were not delayed, he wanted Brian and

Marthe to dine that night. He had so instructed Hector and Melie by airmail, and he expected to see Oliver at the table.

'You too, naturally. Keep the evening free,' Brian told Lauren. 'It will be by way of a celebration.'

'Is Mia Sumner coming back with him?' Lauren could not help asking. But Brian had nothing to pass on about Mia, surmising that as Dale hadn't mentioned her she would probably have stopped off or flown direct to Barbados.

Oliver agreed to be of the party and himself invited Cherry. Hector, deprived by Brian of his right to meet and chauffeur 'the Mister' home, took out his frustration by bullying the gardeners and the houseboy. Melie revelled in the chance to prepare a meal worthy of the occasion, and Lauren, who before Dale's departure hadn't spent more than a quarter of an hour alone with him since that humiliating scene in the cave, did her best to arrange the day of his arrival so that they needn't meet until other people were there—Brian or Marthe or anyone who knew nothing of the undertow of her embarrassment with him.

She spent the morning in an assessment of her wardrobe with a view to its suitability or otherwise to her need of it in England. Handsome shoes, sports wear, evening things—she could sell *those* and *that* and *that*, and buy instead something serviceable off the peg for the rest of an alleged English summer and the threat of winter to come. But tonight, what should she wear for what might be her last social occasion if Oliver were to leave for England quite soon? She found herself with a foolish but irresistible urge to look her best, to dress up in character with her supposed wealth; to recreate the sophistication she had lately discarded in her professional role; to flaunt again the cool *mondaine* poise which had deceived and so enraged Dale that first evening on board *Chaconia Lady*.

To Brian and Marthe and the others she might appear overdressed for a dinner-party of six at home. But no matter—— Brian, her intuition told her, would probably guess she had needed to impress Dale with such a last gesture of opulence, and when she had gone he could tell the sorry little tale to Marthe of how Cinderella had managed not to get found out ...

She decided to wear a slimly-cut scarlet dinner-gown, perfect for her gipsy colouring (... 'put you in a red and orange bandanna ...') but which she had worn only once or twice at the hotel, feeling it to be too garish in competition with the island's own vivid colours. She would wear no jewellery—her windfall hadn't run to rubies!—but her sun-bronzed skin was all that a gipsy's should be without benefit of make-up except a dark shadowing for her eyes.

She purposely made and kept a late enough hairdressing appointment to enable her to go straight to her room to change on her return. There were no cars on the drive at that time and Hector's information was that he should not expect Dale and his guests for another hour. 'Mister Oliver and Missis Huppert down at cottage. Come up later, he say.'

The sun had gone down in grey and gold-barred splendour and the early Caribbean evening had set in before Brian's car drove up and Lauren watched from her window—Brian and Marthe in evening things, Dale to disappear alone into the house, followed by Hector, chattering eagerly and arming luggage with octopus-like dexterity. Lauren gave Dale time to get to his room, and then went down to greet Brian and Marthe, already being plied with drinks by Melie.

Marthe came forward to kiss her. '*Chérie*, you look a million dollars!' she praised. 'But you are a bad, bad girl. Why *will* you not stay on with us? Brian says he can't persuade you, even though, if you wanted to work, he could find you plenty of cases as interesting as Oliver's.'

Lauren took a rum punch from Melie's tray. She shook her head. 'No, I'd planned to move on when Oliver didn't need me any more. I told you so, didn't I?' she appealed to Brian.

'Unfortunately!'

'And you won't stay longer, just for a holiday without working or meaning to? Come to us?' Marthe pressed.

'It's dear of you to ask me,' said Lauren, touched. 'But I've been out of England for far longer than I meant to be and it—calls.'

'One could wish it didn't shout so loud,' Marthe grumbled, as Oliver and Cherry came in, Oliver walking with the aid of only one stick, and Cherry as proudly watchful of him as if he were a robot of her own invention. The small diversion of their arrival and their choosing of drinks brought Brian to Lauren's side. Under cover of his wife's bright chatter to the others he said, 'Something I have to tell you——'

She looked her surprise at the urgency of his tone. 'Something? What?'

He opened his mouth to speak, and then, 'No—later,' he said. 'If I get a chance, some time before we go,' and looking up Lauren saw that his check had coincided with Dale's arrival in the room.

Across it, she looked him straight in the eye, conscious of his appraisal of her appearance, wondering whether it could convey to him the message which her despair dictated—that they had finished with each other, were at an end, and would soon be going their separate ways.

He gave no sign but of acknowledgement of her. Cherry claimed his attention for Oliver, whose truculent question, 'And so, if they've laid on the fatted calf over there, when does the prodigal go and eat it?' Dale answered evenly with, 'When he is willing to go; when his doctor says he should; when'—his glance flicked to Lauren—'his physiotherapist has done with him all she can.'

'Uh-huh—handed over to another sawbones and another trick-cyclist? And who is going to minister to my invalid needs on the way over?'

'You aren't going to *have* any invalid needs,' interposed Cherry vigorously. 'And even if you have, aren't I giving up three weeks of my holiday to fly back with you, you ungrateful hound?'

'You?' Oliver scorned. 'The last time I flew with you, you were airsick. On a day-flip from Ramsgate to Dieppe,' he added cruelly.

'That was different. It was ages ago, and I'd had sausages for breakfast——' They continued to bicker while the others talked over their drinks. Mia was not mentioned. Brian would already have asked Dale about her, and neither of them would expect Lauren to have any curiosity as to where she was, or where Dale and she had parted company. Or whether—Lauren remembered suddenly Brian's strange urgency just now—whether he had been going to tell her that Dale and Mia had returned engaged, a happening which Brian had once told her he would deplore. And *Brian* didn't know the truth of the guilty secret which Mia and Dale and Oliver shared! So how much more would he hate the entanglement for Dale, if he ever learned it?

They dined on the terrace by the light of wall-fixed lanterns, the round table making the talk general. To question Brian Lauren would have had to speak to him across it, and in any case she had sensed that what he had to tell her was for her hearing alone. The ways and means of Oliver's departure and subsequent treatment and convalescence were discussed, and she supposed that as a celebration the gathering was a fair success. But that was largely due to Cherry's ebullient, infectious high spirits. She bullied Oliver into some response to her teasing, and Melie's menu and Dale's choice of wine helped, but there were still threads of tension running between individuals. Between herself and Brian, with his message still untold, between Oliver and Dale as always, though less so lately, between herself and Dale. Or was she perhaps wrong about that, the thread running only from her to him, whatever hostile emotions she had aroused in him having shrunk to an indifference no less punishing where she was concerned?

The night was warm and they stayed on the terrace watching the moon rise. When Cherry's aunt's driver came by car to fetch her, she made him wait, insisting that they all see Oliver to the cottage first.

On the way, having had a helping arm rejected by Oliver with a growl of, 'Unhand me, woman; I'd rather travel under my own steam, thank you,' Cherry had taken Dale's arm instead.

'Didn't Mia Sumner go over to England when you went?' she asked him. 'Where have you dumped her since? Or not?'

Lauren held her breath. Dale said, 'She didn't come back. She stayed.'

'In *England*?' Lauren experienced the same dismay as she heard in Cherry's voice, knowing they shared the same thought—Mia in England, Oliver going home to England and Dale there almost as often as in St Just, amounted to an explosive triangle no less dangerous to their secret than out here.

Dale said, 'No, not in England. She was moving on.'

'Oh! Where to?'

'South Africa.'

'Hoots! Why South Africa?'

'Her people came from there out to Barbados. She met some friends in England and went back with them.'

'For a holiday?'

'I wouldn't know,' Dale said shortly, his tone so dismissing that Cherry gave up.

Lauren wondered. He might have been reporting on a stranger's affairs instead of on Mia, to whom he had been so close that less than a year ago he had voluntarily taken her guilt on to his own shoulders and involved his brother in the continuing lie. Little as any of it would concern her in the future, Lauren sensed that Cherry's curiosity had probed a situation between him and Mia which he had no intention of discussing with Cherry or anyone else.

As every night, Hector was at the cottage, ready to help Oliver to bed. While Cherry unlinked from Dale to speak to Hector, Lauren found herself in momentary isolation with Oliver.

'Get yourself a seat on my flight when I go?' he asked.

'Oh! But I shall probably have gone sooner,' she said. 'In a few days, I expect.'

'What's the hurry? You're not a wage slave, having to clock in to time, are you?'

'No, but—Anyway, you'll have Cherry with you, she told you, and I should think Dale too.'

'"Old Uncle Tom Cobley and all——" in fact. I'd have thought you'd want to be in on handing over the body as your *chef d'oeuvre,*' he sulked.

She had to laugh. 'Don't flatter yourself! You're not my first, and if I should practise again I hope you won't be my last success—even if I've the right to claim you at all.'

'But you'll keep in touch? You took me on; you

can't let Doc down by not following me up!'

Lauren saw the danger ahead. 'If I stay in England,' she promised. 'But this trip has given me a taste for travel which I didn't know I had, and I've a feeling I may move on somewhere else quite soon.'

Oliver turned away. 'In other words, you don't want to know,' he accused her childishly.

That was Oliver, aggrieved and self-pitying to the last. But Lauren mustn't blame him, and for all her brusquerie with him, Cherry didn't. And with Cherry he was in loving hands.

CHAPTER TEN

THEY walked back to the house, leaving Oliver in Hector's care. When Cherry had left, Dale invited Brian and Marthe in for a nightcap. But though Brian seemed inclined to accept, giving Lauren hope that they might manage the private word he wanted with her, Marthe refused for them both and urged him on their way. All the evening there had been four people like a kind of safe padding between herself and Dale, Lauren thought, alone with him now and wanting, yet not wanting to escape. Her goodnight to him was met with a nod.

She walked ahead of him across the hall and had a hand on the newel post of the staircase when his sharp 'No!' halted her and in a stride he was at her back, his own hand propelling her into the long room which gave on to the terrace. There he turned upon her.

'Sit down,' he ordered, and then with scorn, 'You can cut the injured surprise. It's patently not genuine, since Brian will have warned you what to expect.'

'Brian? Warned me? I haven't seen him alone to speak to, for him to give me any warning,' she denied.

Dale's raised brows expressed his doubt. 'He had time enough, and if not, I'd have expected him to make some. Are you quite sure he didn't come straight to you with the story? Phoned you at least, promising his continuing support if I turned savage?'

She shook her head. 'I don't know what you're talking about. Though yes, I admit Brian did say he needed to talk to me——'

'Ah!'

'But he hadn't a chance all the evening.'

'Nor called you earlier?'

'No.' In face of this stony disbelief in her word, her guard broke down. 'Dale, what *is* it?' she pleaded, and as soon as she spoke she thought she knew.

Brian had betrayed her, and he had *promised*! No one, he had sworn, should hear the truth of her paltry masquerade from him. Yet he must have told Dale; told him when he only needed to keep her secret for a few days longer. How *could* he? He had pretended to understand, had even called her courageous ... Somewhere in the back of her mind there was an inkling that had she trusted Brian more by letting him guess that it wasn't her pride but her enduring love which would suffer at Dale's hands, Brian would have gone to the stake to keep faith with her. She had had only to say, 'I love Dale, and I'd only not care about his knowing about my trick, if he loved me. But he doesn't'—and Brian, under no illusions about Mia, would perhaps have understood.

Dale was speaking. He said, 'All right. If you really haven't had the lowdown from Brian, then you must have it from me.' He moved to sit on the arm of a chair, facing her at a foot or so's distance from her. 'You know, I daresay, that in England, after probate has been granted, the will of anyone may be inspected by any other member of the public who wants to enquire about its contents?'

Wonderingly, 'Yes?'

'And I've been over in England,' he said heavily.

Light glimmered for an instant. She moistened her lips. 'And so?'

'And so, as a curious member of the public examining a certain will, I was surprised by something I found there which, I learned today, didn't surprise Brian Gellhorn at all. Can you guess whose the will was, and why I was surprised?'

He had not 'turned savage', but this taut control of his words was no less a menace. Lauren said, 'Since you're telling me about it, I think the will may have been my husband's. But what was your concern with it, and how did you trace it?'

'In the usual way. You'd told me when, approximately, he died and I was able to narrow my search in the records to a presumed three months either way. And my motives were personal, since I don't care, any more than the next man, for being fooled.'

So he had learned the truth for himself; she could not blame Brian, who could only have wanted to tell her he hadn't been able to guard her from Dale's scorn of her at his own discovery of her subterfuge. When she said nothing, looking straight ahead past him, he went on, 'I read that, by his will, Steven Napier left his widow the proceeds of just one life policy. How much?—a thousand pounds, perhaps two?—and the rest of whatever fortune he had to leukaemia research, and though naturally I couldn't learn what that amounted to, you would have known?'

It was Lauren's turn to surprise him. 'Yes, of course. In total, his assets were the current cash in our joint account which came to me, and his personal effects. A life pension he had died with him. I'm afraid the anti-leukaemia campaign didn't benefit very much, though he meant well. Compared with anything else he was able to leave, his legacy to me was a fortune. Would you like to know the exact figure, give or take a few odd pence? You weren't far out in your guess at the amount. It was——'

Dale cut in on that. 'Whatever miserable sum it was, you treated it as if it were a fortune. Why? Had he had money and gone through it? Or did you know when you married him that there would be nothing for you when he died?'

'He hadn't ever been rich, and our marriage was very—frugal.' (In more ways than one, her memory added). 'And yes, I knew I should get very little at his death. Which is why what I did get looked like a fortune to me—a fortune to be spent and not regretted when it was gone, on all the things I'd gone without for years, or had never dreamed of having. And so it bought—oh, a luxury one-way ticket to the Caribbean, and clothes and cosmetics and facials and hair-do's, and parties and no responsibilities for as long as it lasted——'

'—And men's admiration and women's envy and the deliberate fooling of people for whom you didn't give a damn. Fooling the lot of us with malice aforethought—with the exception of Brian, whom you let under your guard and swore him into complicity in the whole ridiculous enterprise,' Dale taunted.

'I didn't set out to fool you,' she denied. 'It just happened that you were there.'

'Exactly. I was "there".'

'Concluding things about me which weren't true, and never had been! That being kind to Lucille meant more to me than—than loving you; that I was a born do-gooder, not a—woman, and that in marrying Steven for pity, I still had an eye on his supposed wealth as a fringe benefit, marked with my name and "Collect". How, tell me that, *how* in the name of anyone's common pride do you suppose I would admit to you that it was all a sham?' she accused him.

Dale said slowly, 'Considering our past relationship, I'd have thought there were ways in which you could have shown me I was jumping to conclusions about you.'

'When?' she demanded hotly. 'When would you have listened or believed me? That first night on board? Did you really expect me to crumple and confess and plead to you, in the black mood you were in? That night I could have *crept* to you, and you would have let me; enjoyed letting me—— And afterwards, it was too late. Afterwards, when I understood about Mia Sumner, I realised it wouldn't matter to you whether I told you the truth or not. And when I'd spent all I had and gone home, it wasn't going to matter to me either.'

'But until then it was important to you to keep your secret from me?'

'And from anyone else on board or here.'

'From anyone? Brian has the strong impression you wanted it kept especially from me.'

'He's mistaken. I didn't say so.' On the defensive, she flared, 'He had no right to discuss it with you at all! I'd *trusted* him——!'

'If he'd had a chance tonight he would have told you I winkled the truth out of him, when my own guesswork and the sight of that will only needed the filling of a few gaps. However, what was it that you "understood" about Mia? You've listened to island gossip and used your own eyes and ears to add two and two to make five?'

Lauren said drily, 'If I did, Mia helped with that arithmetic by warning me off any romantic ideas about you. She hinted that designs on you must have been my ulterior motive for taking Oliver's case.'

'Though I'm sure you hastened to put her right on that?'

'I did——'

'Yet she was justified in wondering, considering that, at the end of your fortnight's indulgence at Le Marechal, you could have escaped with your secret intact.'

'Brian had persuaded me it was my duty to try to help Oliver.'

Dale nodded. 'Ah, your duty. That *would* count with you—as always. But weren't you courting the danger of my finding you out when you agreed we should share the same roof while you were treating him?'

'Yes, I knew the risk,' she agreed.

'Knew it, but took it? Odd, that. To an outsider, as odd as my pressure on you to work from here, wouldn't he think?'

'Odd? Even Brian thought it was reasonable that I should.'

'Just as well. I wasn't going to let you refuse.'

'I know. I had no choice.'

There was a beat of silence. Then Dale said with quiet emphasis, 'Nor had I.'

Lauren brought her gaze to his. 'You? Of course you had. There was no need to invite me here.'

She watched him lever himself from the chair-arm and move to stand in front of her, looking down into her puzzled face. In a difficult, half-choked tone he said, 'I wanted you here, Lauren. I can't pare it down more simply than that. Or can I? Forget the "here". I *wanted* you. Do you understand?'

Her stare at him was fixed, cruelly fascinated. 'No,' she said. 'You haven't wanted me for a very long time. And if you ever did, you wouldn't have let me go.'

'You went. It was an "either–or" thing and you chose Lucille.'

'Because I couldn't desert her, and I couldn't burden you with her at the beginning of your career.'

'And when dear stepmama deserted *you*, why didn't you get in touch again then?'

She sighed. 'It had been too long. You would have stopped even wondering about me by then.'

'Stopped? When I saw you in the Halcyon office, why do you think I pulled strings to get you your passage on *Chaconia Lady*?'

Cornered, 'Well, you did say I had roused your curiosity,' she admitted.

'*And* my hunger for you. And my jealousy. And my hatred of the man who'd had you and turned you into your couturier's model and your hair-dresser's freak.' Dale had drawn her to her feet and taken her into his arms. 'The money that had done this, for instance'—his hand plucked at the draped cleavage of the scarlet gown—'and this'—the hand went to tangle and ruffle the carefully sculptured dressing of her hair. '*I* could have done as much for you if that was what you wanted. But with me you wouldn't have changed from the gipsy-coloured girl I fell in love with into something with as much warm blood in her veins as a Tussauds wax figure. Yes, that first night on board I think I hated you almost as much as I did your Steven.'

Beneath her hands, imprisoned against the mus-cularity of his chest, Lauren could feel his heart beating, thudding the incredible message of a desire to which her own heart was throbbing back its answer. She drew even closer, straining against the hard rock of his body. She murmured, 'I was the same girl. I—still am. Brian understood what deprivation of the good things of life can do to make a girl snatch—at pretties, and appreciation and a little brief power. So can't you?'

He said, 'I've been trying all day, since Brian showed me the fool I've been for judging you. I'm still trying, and with you in my arms it gets easier.' He put a forefinger under her chin. 'You're worried about Mia, aren't you? Jealous of her without cause?'

'*With* cause, surely?' The thought of Mia and his involvement with her dropped like a plummeting stone between herself and Dale. And even if he could convince her they hadn't been lovers, there was still that secret they shared with Oliver, believing it was safe. Lauren shivered and Dale's hand went to her waist.

'Come and sit down and let me tell you about Mia.'

Seated beside her, he did not hold her. While he talked it was for Lauren as if Mia were between them, keeping them apart.

He began, 'If Mia meant anything to me, why do you suppose I haven't chased after her to South Africa, mad with jealousy of the man she's followed out there? A flame of her pre-Barbados days; in diamonds in a big way, and with the wedding ring at the ready, the minute she says Yes.'

'You think she won't be coming back?'

'Perhaps to say "Hi" to her people and the rest of us, that's about all.' Dale went on, 'She began for me when her father started to use Halcyon Line ships for his exports of fruit and sugar to England. That meant we were in frequent business contact, and Mia, at a loose end before she'd made many friends, was always around and latching on to me. I wasn't unwilling. She sparkled—a looker and a turner of heads, exhibitionist to her fingertips, a daredevil in everything from sport to risky love affairs on the surface, and an utter cringing coward underneath. Over the years I've helped her out of one sleazy situation after another—impossible men, scandals she's put about, experiments in soft drugs from which I hauled her almost literally by her beautiful hair. That did frighten her for a time. But she was soon at it again—fast cars, this time, and it wasn't long before she'd bought it in Barbados with two convictions for dangerous driving. In one case she'd injured a child, and Pa Sumner, who was a parent of the ogre class, was fit to be tied with rage. And of course mine was the shoulder she chose, as always, to cry on.'

'But knowing how she was using you, you didn't break with her? You've even had her stay over while I've been here,' Lauren reminded him.

'Business-wise, I couldn't break with her father, and I'd learned not to provoke her spite, as other people's reputations have learned to their cost. Besides, when I invited her to stay this last time, she was frightened. Frightened to her backbone, though concealing it superbly, and I had to pity her.'

'And help her again?' Lauren asked stonily.

'I'd already done that. This was a hangover from some months back, from last year when Oliver was smashed up.' Dale paused. 'This is something you aren't going to like, but I owe you the truth. You'll have heard the public version of the accident—that I admitted crashing the car and took the rap for it. But in fact Mia was at the wheel, though no one but Oliver and I knew she was with us—until now, that is, now that I've told you.'

Lauren shook her head. '*Not* until now. I knew it already.'

Frowning, Dale stared at her. 'How could you? How? Who——?'

She told him. At the end he commented, 'So Oliver cracked at last! Mia was increasingly terrified that he might, and knowing how he despised her for sheltering behind me, I knew there was always a chance that he would. Which made a major reason for my getting him to England and off her back.'

And she had believed his anxiety to send Oliver home had stemmed at least partially from his need to be rid of her, thought Lauren as Dale asked, 'Has Oliver spread the story around—told anyone other than Cherry?'

'No,' Lauren told him. 'Cherry thinks he only told her because he was so tired of carrying around the guilt that he had to tell someone in order to slough it off. But it won't go further. I think Cherry wants to forget it as soon as she can, and Oliver doesn't know she's told even me.'

'Not that it matters so much now, now that Mia has successfully escaped the scandal, and he can leave the guilt behind him. Such guilt as there was in holding his tongue about Mia's being there, for that was all I asked of him—his silence on that,' Dale added.

But Lauren, out of her need to know him utterly honest with her, made herself question, '*All* you asked of Oliver? Hadn't he to promise to keep quiet about your—perjury too?'

She thought she would never forget the look of mingled recoil and outrage which Dale turned on her. She felt herself shrink inwardly at having doubted him as he echoed, 'Perjury? Mine—on oath? Be careful, Lauren. What kind of a criminal do you think me? Or at least a damned fool—if "criminal" is going too far?'

'I—I've told you the story as I had it from Cherry Huppert,' she stammered. 'Oliver was in the back seat, you were beside Mia, at the wheel and driving like a madwoman on these roads. You shouted at her; she just tossed her head, and Oliver knew nothing more until he was on the grass verge, Mia wasn't there, and you were telling him you'd caused the crash, that you were driving when it happened.'

Dale dded. 'Fair enough. The truth.'

'How could it have been? Mia——'

'—Had no control over the car at the point of crash. Before it I had fought her—literally fought her—for the steering-wheel and the brake. The struggle didn't help, and I got control too late at the speed we were going. But at the point of impact and for some time before, though it may only have been minutes, I was driving. As I told the court.'

Lauren managed a tremulous smile. 'So you and Oliver only had to deny that Mia was with you?'

'If we'd been asked and had denied it, that would have been perjury too. But my warning to Oliver was unnecessary—the question never arose.

We had only to hold our tongues, and naturally Mia held hers. And all that's remained of the whole affair has been the nastiness of her fear of him, and his hatred of her.'

'He hated her for her willingness to shelter behind you, Cherry says,' Lauren offered.

'I suppose her experience of me told her she could.'

'Yes— Dale, tell me—from what you seem to know of her, warts and all, as it were, I don't think you are or have been in love with her, but why were you always there for her when she was in trouble? *Why* could she always run to you?'

Dale answered the question with one of his own. 'Never gone all knight-errant quixotic, brimming milk of human kindness, for someone weaker or sillier or more down on his or her luck—hunkers than yourself? Simply for pity, no more?'

'Ye-es, I suppose I have.'

'Give examples!'

'I don't know that I—— Oh, well, I suppose I did for Lucille.'

'And——?'

She thought. 'You mean—Steven?'

Dale nodded. 'You could add Oliver, though I doubt if you could count him as a prime example. I'd rather hear you made use of him because you wanted to stay on as much as I wanted you to. I'd have been prepared to shanghai you if you'd refused his case. Come here——'

Lauren stayed where she was at the end of the window-seat. 'Only if you admit there's nothing to choose between us when it comes to pity. Yours for Mia, mine for——'

'Come *here*!'

She went then, and when his arms enfolded her again, suddenly Mia wasn't even a shadow. Nor Lucille. Nor Steven. The only realities were Dale and herself, heart to heart.

There was a long searching of each other's faces, a tantalising holding off from the deep intimacies of lips on lips and seeking, demanding hands which would set flesh afire with sensual delight. Then their desire fused and glowed in the crucible of their need and while they breathlessly clung and murmured evergreen little love-words, they were at the mercy of a passion which craved to be assuaged. And for Lauren this time, there was no shame in her invitation to him to lust for her as she did for him, pagan and reckless in her utter committal to him, body and mind.

He had tweaked the long cushion from the window-seat to the floor, had drawn her to kneel there with him, and then had lain beside her. Now he urged thickly, 'Marry me, Lauren! *Marry me*——'

Her fingers gently traced the line of his cheek, lingered at his lips to be kissed. 'Yes,' she said.

'Here and now? Are you ready?'

'Yes,' she said again. 'But do you—— Would you want me to do that?'

There was the lift of eyebrow and twitch of mouth-corner which she had always loved. 'I rather hoped I'd been telling you so!'

'You have. And I understand. But——'

'But you want a ring and a wedding night? And

so, my love, my love, you shall have them. But I warn you, this is the last time I shall get to the point of proposing marriage to you. A man has his limits, after all.'

With his adroit, timely flippancy he had turned a dangerous corner for them both, and she loved him for it. Lightly too, taking her cue, she asked, 'Why, how many other times have there been?'

'Too many. The first you'll remember—when you turned me down in favour of Lucille. And the latest before this—the night I took you to the *boucan* with that purpose.'

She shook her head. 'Oh no. You were still hating me for deceiving you then. And if it hadn't rained, what excuse would you have had for keeping me there? I'd only gone to *see* the cave.'

'The gods were on my side, and it did rain. But then you took the stupid game I'd suggested too far,' he retorted.

'Oh, Dale, if only you'd known I *wasn't* playing! I was trying to make love to you in some way you'd understand. But I failed, and you were cruel, and for sheer pride's sake I had to pretend I was acting!'

'You'd stolen my scene, and I couldn't forgive you for showing you knew so much about inflaming a man without caring for him at all. Believing then, as I've told you, that you couldn't, and perhaps never did, care for me.'

'Yet you'd planned to ask me to marry you?' she prompted.

'I couldn't help myself. I'd reached a point where I had to know.'

She knelt up beside him. 'And if you'd said "Marry me" that night, I'd have snatched—as I was tempted to, just now,' she confessed.

Dale knelt up too, stood and drew her to her feet. 'And now we aren't snatching, knowing that it's all going for us as we both want, will you promise me one thing, my heart?' he urged.

'*Anything!* What?'

'That when we've been patient about reciting our "to have and to hold from this day forward——" and the rest, on our real wedding night will you come with me to the *boucan* and let me marry you there?'

'You mean——?'

'I think you know. Claim you, take you, possess you. Will you come?'

She understood, and felt desire start again within her at the thought of the possession of each other which they would enjoy.

'With a pile of dry bracken fronds for our marriage bed?' she teased fondly.

'And rain, which I shall have ordered, to keep us there until dawn. Or better still, no rain, so that when you tire of my lovemaking, we can go outside and count the stars.'

'*I* shan't tire of making love.'

'Nor I, of learning new tricks from my little gipsy strumpet.'

'She only knows the ones that loving you have taught her——'

He had turned her towards the stairs, and they kept the fantasy going until they reached the door of her room. There he stooped to kiss her softly yielding mouth. 'At least dream of me,' he said.

'I'll try.' But when he had left her, Lauren knew she didn't want either to sleep or to dream. For tonight the reality of loving Dale and being loved by him was going to be enough.

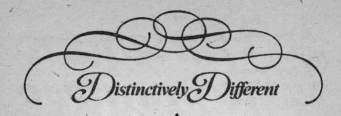

Distinctively Different

Harlequin Presents...

Beautiful love stories that offer
the excitement of exotic places,
warm, true-to-life characters,
and the thrill of romance.

Rare blends of sophistication,
refreshing realism and drama that
let your imagination sweep you into
the special world of love that only
Harlequin can create!

*From the publisher that understands
how you feel about love.*

Harlequin Romances

The books that let you escape
into the wonderful world of romance!
Trips to exotic places...interesting
plots...meeting memorable people...
the excitement of love.... These are
integral parts of Harlequin Romances —
the heartwarming novels read by
women everywhere.

Many early issues are now available.
Choose from this great selection!

Choose from this list of Harlequin Romance editions.*

Some of these book were originally published under different titles.